I'M YOUR VENUS

D1240710

SYLVIA STRYKER
SPACE CASE #2

I'M YOUR VENUS

DIANE VALLERE

Polyester Press

LOS ANGELES | READING

Copyright Page

I'M YOUR VENUS

Sylvia Stryker Novel #2

A Polyester Press Publication

Print ISBN: 9781939197504

Ebook ISBN: 9781939197498

To the staff of the Los Feliz branch of the Los Angeles, Public Library, for giving me an office away from home.

MOON UNIT CREW AND PASSENGER MANIFEST

(Results of background check as conducted by Lt. Sylvia Stryker)

Commander Anatol: Moon Unit Science Officer. Second in command of Moon Unit 6. Two different color eyes.

Astryd, Xina: Venusian. Beautiful. Winner of publicity contest for a ticket to Venus on Moon Unit 6. Seven feet tall.

Bottol: Martian. Little. Green. Male. Communications crew.

Champion, Zeke: Son of spaceship repairman. Expert on hacking and space drone technology. Friend of Sylvia Stryker.

Dusk, Mattix: Space courier. Taught Sylvia Hapkido fighting style in exchange for repairs and modifications to space pod.

Doc Edison: Head of Medi-Bay. Cranky.

Low tolerance for secret missions.

Ellison: son of attaché to Ambassador Reeves. Chaser of Pika. Thrower of ice cream. Causer of stains on soiled uniforms.

George: attaché to Ambassador Reeves.

Lumiere, John: Officer, Independent Border Patrol. Assigned to Moon Unit 6 to enforce Federation Council rule. Overseeing the transport of precious cargo.

Marshall, Vaan: Youngest member of Federation Council. Sylvia's first love. Plunian.

Neptune: Head of security on Moon Unit Corporation. Muscular wall of taciturn authority. Inspires fear in others. Background: maybe better left unknown.

Pika: pink Gremlon alien who has snuck on board the ship. Possible troublemaker.

Qidd, Cheung: Evil space pirate. Serving life sentence on Colony 13 for collusion with Jack Stryker.

Ambassador Reeves, Yesenia: Federation Council ambassador to Venus.

Captain Ryder, Katherine: Captain of Moon Unit 6. Plunian. Role model.

Starr, Ofra: Engineer of Moon Unit 6. Preference for glittery eyeshadow. Note: wears custom uniforms. Dry clean only. Do not shrink!

Stryker, Jack: The prisoner formerly known

as "dad." Currently serving life sentence in Federation Council jail.

Stryker, Sylvia: space academy dropout. Half Plunian and half Human. Has photographic memory, lavender skin, and excellent problem-solving abilities. Grew up on dry ice farm. Hates space pirates. Difficulty breathing unregulated air without bubble helmet. Uniform lieutenant, second class.

Synn: Venusian male. Half of the entertainment duo on Moon Unit 6.

Shyrr: Venusian. Female. Half of the entertainment duo on Moon Unit 6.

Teron, Daila: Former uniform lieutenant. Current Yeoman. Direct responsibility for uniform ward (among other assignments).

Vesta: daughter of a factory worker and a Venusian involved in a government-sanctioned cross-breeding experiment.

Woodward, TJ: personnel director for Moon Unit Corporation. Responsible for filling all jobs on ship.

Zuni, Nyota: hostess in the Space Bar (restaurant on board Moon Unit 6).

Countless unnamed crew members and passengers have been omitted from this list when they were deemed inconsequential to the solving of Space Case #2.

1: DEPARTURE POINT

Moon Unit 6 was twice the size of the last spaceship the company had in rotation, and, thanks to the wonders of technology, half the weight. At least that's what the promotional catalog claimed. The ship was docked by the boarding station where families of sweepstakes finalists were gathered. The sweepstakes was a publicity stunt intended to distract the tourist-traveling public from what had happened the last time a Moon Unit promised "the adventure of a lifetime."

A whole lot had changed for me on that trip, not the least of which was the destruction of my home planet, Plunia. So, while I understood why a lot of the crew who I'd met on my first Moon Unit mission chose to seek employment elsewhere, I had my own motivation for returning to the company. In short, I had nowhere else to go.

"Stryker," said a gruff voice behind me.

I turned to face a wall of muscle dressed in a fitted black T-shirt and a pair of cargo pants. Only one division of the Moon Unit crew wasn't required to wear regulation uniforms on the day of departure: security. But it didn't take the memorization of the uniform regulations to recognize the man approaching me. He was Neptune, the head of the security division. "I wasn't sure you'd be here," he said.

"C'mon, you know you already checked the crew manifests to see if they hired me back. Don't lie on my account."

Neptune raised one eyebrow. It was his signature facial expression. During some of the worst circumstances I'd experienced in my life, the only reaction I'd gotten out of him was a raised eyebrow. "Don't worry, you won't have to bust me this time. I'm an official crew member. See?" I held up the plastic ID that hung from a lanyard around my neck. *Sylvia Stryker, Uniform Lieutenant, 2nd class, Moon Unit 6.*

Neptune took my ID card between his fingers and read it. "You should have applied to work security. You're overqualified for this assignment." He dropped the plastic and it bounced against my chest.

"The employee manual says security positions are only for graduates of the space academy."

"You were supposed to get your degree after Moon Unit 5 docked."

"I got distracted."

Neptune's heavy, eyebrows pulled together over his intensely dark eyes, and he stared at me in a way that probably cracked a lot of criminals. It had a different effect on me. I mean, sure, my pulse picked up and I became aware of my breathing, but not because he made me feel guilty. Something about Neptune challenged me in a way I hadn't been challenged before, and in the months after our last moon trek, I'd found my thoughts returning to the mystery behind the head of security.

Moon Unit 6 had been designed with not one but two lounges from which passengers could literally stare off into space. Today, the crew had been encouraged to board early and assemble on Observation Deck One to watch the sweepstakes festivities. OB One was connected to the ship by a diagonal beam, allowing us to look down on the hopeful passengers from an overhead perspective. Because my Plunian respiratory system required air with a higher oxygen content than humans needed, I wore an air filtration helmet that regulated my intake until the ship passed the breakaway point into zero gravity. At that point, the ship maintained a proprietary blend of nitrogen and oxygen that accommodated the widest range of species. At least on this journey, I wouldn't have to hide my genetic shortcomings. It was hard enough trying to blend in with purple skin.

"Besides," I said, "You're the head of security. If you wanted me to work on your team, you could have contacted me to let me know."

Neptune gestured at the crowds awaiting the announcement. "Moon Unit Corporation kept me busy with this contest. There's a personnel director on the staff. It was up to him to fill vacancies on the crew, not me."

"I met him the day I picked up my uniforms. TJ Woodward, right? Nice guy. A little too clean cut for my tastes, but he didn't make a big deal about my background, so I figured he was okay."

"Your name was on the pre-approved list. Staff of Moon Unit 5 were automatic hires if you applied. After what we went through, it was the easiest way for the company to avoid a lawsuit."

"Who threatened to sue?"

"The Martians."

Figured. From my very first run-in with the little green men, I hadn't been a particularly big fan.

"So, Stryker. Anything I need to know before we depart for Venus?" Neptune asked. "Secrets you plan to keep that will make my job more difficult?"

"No secrets. My name is on the crew manifests. Legitimately this time. And like I told you, the biggest problem I plan to deal with is keeping the crew in clean uniforms. Maybe somebody will spill something and challenge me with a stain. Other than that, I'm just a girl looking for a free trip to Venus."

In terms of tourist destinations, Venus was an interesting choice. It was rumored that the planet's atmosphere triggered amorous feelings in visitors and made it desirable for honeymoons, romantic getaways, and illicit affairs. And since Venus was already zoned for residential colonies and tourist activities, the atmosphere was clear enough for me to breathe.

"No plans to do anything that will require me to lock you up?"

"Nope. I'm going to be the best uniform lieutenant the new Moon Unit owners have ever seen. I passed the physical with flying colors, and I fit everything I need into one bag to minimize the weight print of the ship. If Yeoman D'Nar gives me even a hint of attitude, I'm going to wave my hiring papers in her face."

"Yeoman D'Nar isn't on this trek. She left the company. You didn't run your own background checks?"

"No," I said. "I thought I'd learn about my coworkers the regular way."

Our conversation was cut short when a spokesperson for Moon Unit Corporation took to the stage below the observation deck. Families crowded closer to viewing and listening stations to hear if their loved one was the winner of the I'm Your Venus Promotional Contest.

"How do the announcers know the name they draw is cleared for the trip?" I asked, partially to myself.

"Part of the application process. Each of the finalists signed waivers that said their likeness could be used in the media campaign surrounding the trip."

"What about background checks and physicals? Stuff like that? Moon Unit Corp has been promoting this contest for the past two months. We're scheduled for departure today. How do they know nothing happened in that time to disqualify a person from being eligible?"

"You're overly suspicious," Neptune said.

"You're security section. Aren't you?"

His arms were crossed over his chest, and his feet were shoulder-width apart. It was the Neptune stance. The effect was intentional intimidation and judging from the way non-crew members gave him a wide berth as they passed, it was effective. Just not on me. I'd developed a mental immunity to his tactics somewhere around the point when he risked his position to protect me. I had so many questions about his actions, but I hadn't asked them, and now, after what I'd learned about him during our break, I didn't know if those questions were better left ignored.

And while my brain had questions about Neptune's motivations, my vital signs had an agenda of their own. Whenever I thought about him for any length of time, my purple coloring intensified. Right now, standing next to him for the first time since we'd parted after the last trip, I was thankful for the long sleeves of my uniform.

"There's a list of finalists in the main computer," Neptune said. "I've been monitoring each of them for the past thirty days. Daily routine, job, health, colleagues, financial status. The system pings when one of them so much as puts on an unusually colored pair of socks. Moon Unit Corp wasn't going to take any chances on who they let on board this ship."

"But it's supposed to be random, right? There's a giant fiberglass ball on the stage next to the spokesperson. She's going to spin the ball and then pull a name and announce it in front of all these people. Random."

He leaned closer. My bubble helmet kept me from detecting his scent or feeling his breath on my ear, but I flushed anyway. I pulled my sleeves down over my hands to hide the glow. "That's what they want you to think," he said. He pulled away and raised his eyebrow again.

It made sense that the company would have

some sort of control over their passengers, but I hadn't expected them to fool the general public of our galaxy with something of this magnitude. Once upon a time people may have signed up for a sweepstakes and not thought about the trade-off of their personal information, but after Earth became so overpopulated that earthlings had moved onto other planets, and galaxies that had gone largely undiscovered became fair game for developers, everything changed. Now everybody was looking to make a buck. For some, all it took was a decent bribe and a knowledge of back channels to find out what they wanted to know.

That, I knew firsthand.

My skills with computers and electronics had been my main source of income since the moon trek three months ago. Despite my claims of being on the up and up for the trip to Venus, I'd engaged in more than one illegal act since the last time he'd seen me. A girl's gotta make a living. Even a Plunian.

The general noise level from the dock rose, and chutes released pressurized steam into the sky around the platform. Giant light filters had been angled around the stage, and the steam took on shades of bright yellow, citrine, and chartreuse. For about seventeen seconds, *everybody* looked Martian. And then, a name was projected onto the wall behind the stage: Xina Astryd. A tall woman with shimmery skin that appeared to glow from within strolled toward the stage. Her luminous hair caught the tones of the filters and lit up like filaments. Her deliberate pace didn't fit the excitement of the event or the surroundings, and others in the crowd bent their heads together and whispered as she passed them.

"Is she the winner?" I asked. "She doesn't look particularly happy."

"Xina Astryd. Venusian. Notoriously reserved. Left Venus to pursue a career in the entertainment industry on Colony 7."

"I thought Colony 7 was mostly Gremlons."

"Mostly, but not exclusively."

I wanted Neptune to keep talking, but his focus had shifted from our casual conversation to the platform below. Xina had a regal quality about her, not exactly hurt by the fact that she was seven feet tall—a full head and shoulders above everyone else. Venusians averaged taller height than most aliens in the galaxy, especially the women. Their planet was a decadent vacation spot enjoyed by those with money to burn, and since my home planet had been populated with ice miners and potato farmers, I'd never had the wherewithal to go. Even before space pirates had destroyed it, we'd mostly stayed where we were.

A light on the interior of the observation deck blinked yellow. It was a reminder to general crew to head to our positions for takeoff. I pointed to the lights. "Time to get to our stations. Are you coming?"

If Neptune answered, I didn't hear him. All noise in the observation deck was drowned out by an explosion on the docking deck below.

2: BORDER PATROL

OF THE TWENTY OR SO MOON UNIT CREW
members who had crowded around the windows of
Observation Deck One, all but two dropped to the
floor at the sound of the explosion. Those two were
Neptune and me. Neptune took off for the stairs
with me right behind him. It wasn't until after we
reached the exit that I realized it was his job to
make sure the crowds were safe. Mine was to make
sure they were dressed in the appropriately recognized garments. And even after remembering that,
I didn't stop myself from trying to help. It was a
man in an unfamiliar white uniform who stopped
me instead.

The man at the ship exit had brown skin and
bright green eyes. His white hat covered his head
and buckled under his chin, keeping his hair color a
mystery. I could identify any of the crew members

according to their uniform, but this man's wasn't one of ours. It had black fabric lining the collar, cuffs and trim down the front. A white patch with "IBP" was stitched onto the left side. There was no point trying to argue my way past this him. He was with the Independent Border Patrol.

I'd heard rumors that Moon Unit Corp had contracted with an independent company to clear passengers on the ship, but until this moment hadn't known the rumors were true.

"Lieutenant," he said. "You can't leave."

"But there's a security situation on the docking platform," I said. "People are in danger."

"You're security?" He glanced at my uniform—magenta with silver trim. Far removed from the utilitarian look of the black security section outfit Neptune wore.

"No, I'm the uniform lieutenant. There was an explosion, and the head of security might need help with the crowds. My background is in security."

His eyes swept me again, this time taking in my bubble helmet and lavender skin. "Stryker, right?"

"Right. Lieutenant Sylvia Stryker."

"Officer Lumiere."

I pointed to the patch on his jacket. "I heard a rumor about IBP. Moon Unit Corporation isn't taking any chances this time, are they?"

"New ownership. Aside from the name 'Moon Unit,' everything is different."

"Not everything. The alarm codes and the uniforms and the Space Bar—"

Lumiere cut me off. "You were on Moon Unit 5, weren't you?"

I nodded.

"Then you understand how important it is that Moon Unit 6 runs like clockwork. Trust me when I say there are eyes everywhere." He pointed to the docking platform. "No one is in danger. That explosion was simply a canister of citron atoms fired into the atmosphere to celebrate the contest and send off the ship."

"But it sounded like an explosion. And the head of security acted like it was an explosion."

"The festivities were planned by the entertainment purser. He tested everything he could while maintaining the surprise. The only thing he couldn't test was the sound level."

I looked at the horizontal beams of light that created a barrier by the ship entrance and exit. Neptune had charged past the threshold before the beams had activated and now stood on the other side. Despite the explanation by Lumiere, I was shaken by the seriousness of Neptune's expression. If everything the border patrol agent said was true, then Neptune would have known about the explosion ahead of time, and that it represented no threat. He was the kind of guy who acted first and explained later. It was the most important skill of a good security guard, more than anything that could be taught in a lecture hall or tested for on an entrance exam, and despite the skeletons I'd discovered in Neptune's closet, heroics were in his genes.

I moved to the window for a better view of the stage. While Neptune looked at the crowd from their level, I watched from above like the eye in the sky. Xina had slowly made her way to the left of the stage where Neptune stood. He held out his hand, and she took it and stepped down gracefully until they were on the same level. She was taller than he was, but his muscular build helped maintain his air of authority. He dropped her hand and guided her off the stage.

The air was green. Exploding citron capsules can do that. A sparkly luster coated everyone below. Holographic images were projected at spots around the exterior, and the iridescent light particles that hadn't attached to the crowd floated like the halo effect of an asteroid field with electrostatic properties. It was beautiful.

A young boy ran through the crowd, leaving a trail of sparkly chartreuse space dust circling in his wake. He chased what appeared to be a small pink critter—cat or dog or—oh, no. That wasn't a critter. That was Pika, a playful Gremlon who had stowed away on the previous moon trek. And while I knew the pink alien girl held no threat other than possible distraction, I also knew there was no way a

Gremlon who'd hitchhiked from Colony 7 to the space station and hid onboard the ill-fated Moon Unit 5 would produce the proper credentials to get past Independent Border Patrol.

Like most Gremlons, Pika was a barrel of fun. But the entertainment company that had bought the company had planned out the onboard entertainment, and there'd been no mention of her.

I watched as Pika scampered between viewing stations and vanished. The boy who chased her stopped short, dropped down to his hands and knees and peeked between fixtures, legs, and luggage for her. A man in a blue space jumpsuit picked the boy up by his collar and set him on his feet. While the man shook his finger in the boy's face, I scanned the ground for Neptune or Pika. I'd lost track of both.

Officer Lumiere left his position guarding the door and came over to me. "Lieutenant Stryker," he said, "Personnel is requested to take their stations."

"Why would you know that, and I wouldn't?"

He pointed up. "Announcement over the speakers. Between the noise on the platform and your helmet, you didn't hear."

"Do what the border patrol agent says," said Neptune's voice. He was nowhere near me, which made the verbal communication all the more startling.

I'd been waiting for Neptune to use the

communication device that had been part of my orientation and gear packet. I recognized the equipment for what it was and didn't know it wasn't standard for all crew members. My friend, Zeke Champion, who I'd spent the past couple of months hanging out with, hacked into the channel, only to discover nobody else was on the network. It was only then that I suspected it was black ops issue. And there was only one person I knew who was both Moon Unit employed and had access to black ops equipment.

I'd tried to contact Neptune using the device but received the error message, "out of range." Removing it required a medical procedure and I doubted Neptune would have appreciated the breach in security. Zeke, I could trust. And just to be sure, I paid him off.

But if there'd been any question about whether Neptune planned on using the comm to communicate, the question was now answered. I clenched my teeth together and balled up my fists. Just hearing his voice invading the personal space of my bubble helmet told me he planned to keep me under his thumb.

I made a show of releasing the clamps on my helmet and pulling it off. "Thank you," I said to Lumiere. "I'll be more attentive in the future."

He nodded once. I headed to the staff entrance. When I was certain no one was paying attention to me, I activated the comm device again. "I thought this thing was for emergencies?"

"It's a comm device. It's for communication."

"How come you waited until now to test it?"

"It doesn't need testing."

"But you never used it before."

"It only works up to a certain distance. I activated it when you came on board."

Lucky me. "Why are you giving me orders? I don't report to you."

"I'm surveilling the IBP agent, and I don't want to give him any reasons to act on his own."

"The whole point of the Independent Border Patrol is that they're independent. Why are you surveilling him?" I got out of line and stood to the side, waving fellow crew members past.

"It's rumored that Moon Unit 6 is carrying precious cargo."

"In addition to the passengers? What?"

"Classified."

I lowered my voice. "That's an easy way of saying you don't trust me."

"Over and out."

"Well, that's just great," I said. Neptune didn't respond.

Moon Units were cruise ships, and the new owners were calling the shots. That meant a lean crew to pilot and navigate the ship and a robust staff to attend to the needs of our paying passengers. Entertainment director, food and beverage staff, certified aestheticians and masseurs at the Celestial Spa, manager of the Space Bar, Ion 54, and Cafeteria 15, where our gourmet chef prepared meals using the fifteen rare earth elements in the Lanthanide series to spice up otherwise bland space food.

The metallic earth elements hadn't been considered for ingestion until a scientist discovered the shavings boosted immunity to trace (and toxic) metals found in common foods. Having grown up on a farming planet, I'd been relatively safe from metal poisoning and hadn't had a reason to sample the Lanthanide series, but I'd discovered a particular affinity for the yttrium burger. The side effects were similar to a booster shot of iron, which was only affordable to the wealthier residents of the galaxy.

I went to the end of a small line of crew waiting to pass through the transition chamber. In front of me stood a large, black man with silver eyeshadow, burgundy lip gloss, and expertly contoured cheeks. His hair was shorn close to his scalp and a thin side-part had been shaved into it.

"Do not tell me they plan to bombard my custom uniform with chemicals," he said. He waved his hand back and forth in front of his face as if something smelled. I considered pulling my helmet back on.

"They won't," I said. "The sanitizing chambers eliminated 99.99999 percent of all allergens from space, and anybody already on the ship passed through the deionization chamber before reaching OB One."

The man turned. "How do you know that?"

"It was on the publicity material." I smiled. "I wanted to know everything about the ship that I could."

"Ofra Starr," the man said. He smiled, revealing teeth that had been embedded with diamond chips. He held out his hand, fingertips pointed down. I shook them as best as I could. "I'm the engineer. What's your assignment?"

"Uniform ward."

Ofra's smile vanished. "I trust you spent as much time learning about the proper care of fabrics as you did about the ship? My uniforms were tailored by artisans."

"I'm an expert on all things uniform," I said with confidence.

"I'll be the judge of that," he said.

We passed through the transition chamber and stepped onto the ship. Ofra went one direction and I went the other. I was more interested in the oxygenated air inside. The sooner I could shed the oxygen canister strapped to my waist, the sooner my uniform would be a little less snug. I turned right at the intersection of Sector 7 and Sector 8 and, in about a hundred feet, entered the uniform ward.

My employment history with Moon Unit Corporation was colored by the lies I'd told to get a job. I knew I was qualified to work on a spaceship. I'd almost graduated from the space academy—I *would have* graduated from the space academy—if my dad hadn't been arrested for colluding with space pirates and I had to drop out. But I was smart, and just because I wasn't being tested or graded on my knowledge anymore didn't mean I wasn't going to keep learning.

I logged my arrival time and initial findings into the daily log. Then I put my bubble helmet and oxygen canister on the top shelf of the inventory closet. Just as I was about to commence with the daily tally of uniforms, the doors swished open and a sweetly attractive, pale woman with features similar to my own entered. I'd never met her face to face, but I'd know her anywhere. She was Daila Teron, the crew member whose credentials I'd sabotaged to fake my way on the last trip.

Cue my first problem.

3: DAILA TERON

"Lieutenant Stryker," Daila said.

In a nanosecond, my brain processed her blue uniform with the Moon Unit 6 insignia stitched into the fabric and the single black band around the wrist of her sleeve and computed her rank.

"Yeoman Teron," I said.

She seemed annoyed that I wasn't surprised by her arrival. "I thought we should meet." She held her hand out formally.

I shook it but said nothing. Until Daila either thanked me for solving the murder of her brother or attacked me for stealing her credentials, I wasn't sure where we stood. I could see things going either way.

"Neptune speaks highly of you," she said. "He said you two work well together."

A surprising third option. "My education was in security. Assisting him was second nature."

"He said."

"I'm here as the uniform lieutenant. I don't anticipate stepping into a security role on our trip to Venus."

"I'm happy to hear that."

While my brain fired the synaptic message of *does not compute!,* I called on everything I knew about Moon Unit 6, the vacant positions, the skillset of Daila, and why she'd talked to Neptune about my job performance. And then, I realized there was one Yeoman I knew who wasn't returning for this voyage. Yeoman D'Nar. Who'd been my last boss.

"You took over for Yeoman D'Nar?" I asked.

"Moon Unit Corporation suppressed information on the ranking officers on the ship this time. To prevent having any unscreened aliens from using our background to sneak on board."

So that's how it was gonna be.

Sure, to Daila, I was an alien from Plunia. But in reality, I was only half alien. My dad's half. Which made me hate him even more for destroying our lives. But Plunians were unemotional and detached, and in a case like this, I needed that genetic makeup. Daila could insult me as much as she wanted; I'd heard worse.

"Are you here for the pre-flight check?" I asked.

Her gaze swept the interior of the room. When the new Moon Unit was designed, attention had been paid to minimizing the footprint of all janitorial and storage areas, and uniforms somehow got relegated to that category. Thus, the new uniform ward was half the size of the old one. In addition to the inventory closet, there was a cabinet of contaminant-resistant uniforms for those with top-level security clearance, a wall-mounted computer, and a row of cleaning machines. A laundry bin sat below a chute that sent soiled garments from anywhere on the ship to here for sanitizing.

I should have applied for the security position.

"The ward looks to be in order—for now. The Book of Protocols recommends unscheduled checks of all of my areas of responsibility, so I'm sure you'll see me again." She turned to leave.

"Yeoman Teron," I said. She turned back. "Since I am your direct report, do you have any specific direction for me? I'd like you to be clear with your expectations from the get-go to avoid any potential clashes."

She seemed surprised by my request. "You do your job and let the rest of the crew do theirs. Learn the BOP. Stay out of the way of paying passengers. You're my responsibility, Lieutenant, I won't let you get away with what Yeoman D'Nar did." She turned around and left.

I hadn't had a particularly good relationship

with my last boss, and it looked as though things weren't going to change. Didn't matter. My goal was to do my job, make professional connections, and advance through the ranks of the ship as positions became available. It would be a long road to getting the kind of title I'd always dreamed of, especially since I hadn't completed my degree, but I'd get it eventually. I was qualified for any job on this ship aside from the senior level officers, and slowly but surely, I would prove my worth.

One thing I didn't have to worry about was learning the BOP. The Book of Protocols covered policy, procedure, and expected behavior of every member of the crew. The new owners hadn't left much room for interpretation, including timetables for meals, lights out, and crew mingling. There was an entire chapter on uniform expectations, and it wasn't a stretch to expect me to be familiar with the content. Not only had I memorized that chapter, I'd memorized the entire BOP. All five hundred and twenty-nine pages of it. Moon Unit 5's BOP was only two hundred and thirty-seven pages. Which indicated both the loquaciousness of the current author and the boredom level I'd achieved between jobs.

This being departure day, there wasn't much for me to do. Not knowing I had the BOP committed to memory, Daila had probably thought that project would keep me busy. For all I knew, she was going to quiz me tomorrow. I pressed my hand onto the touchpad of the wall-mounted computer, stood still for an ocular scan that verified my identity and rank, and cued up the file. It was like reading the updated edition of an old, favorite book.

"Stryker," barked a voice in my ear.

"What do you want?" I asked.

"There's a disturbance in Sector 12," Neptune said.

"Does this disturbance have to do with someone being out of uniform? Because that's my job. You're in charge of security."

"The disturbance has to do with a certain pink Gremlon who's been cornered by Martians. Pika's in danger."

And...cue problem number two.

4: MARTIAN TROUBLE

ANOTHER PERSON MIGHT HAVE ASKED WHY Neptune called me. Checking on a disturbance didn't fall under the scope of my official job, and no doubt there was someone else on the ship to whom it did. But even though my responsibilities related to those pertaining to uniforms, my instincts ran toward protecting those who needed help. And Pika fell into that category.

I'd first met Pika on Moon Unit 5. It had been impossible not to like her. It wasn't until after the moon trek was over that I learned she had the same effect on Neptune. She'd followed him to the spaceship from his ranch on the Kuiper Belt where she'd been squatting, and he looked the other way when she snuck on board. It would have been nice to spend time with her, even if she was a Gremlon

36

who lacked the ability to understand genuine remorse, guilt, and loyalty.

There were two ways to get to Sector 12 from the uniform ward: the publicly approved, well-lit, series of interconnected hallways that every other passenger and crew member on Moon Unit 6 would use to mingle, and the High Velocity Pressure Transport system. The HVPTS was a narrow tube that exploded with a pressurized charge and launched anyone in the chamber from one point of the ship to another. It was designed for use by the security staff and top-level crew and hadn't been mentioned on the illustrations of the ship that were part of Moon Unit Corporation's publicity campaign. The only reason I knew about it was because I'd downloaded the schematics from the mainframe a week before departure. When it comes to escape routes, a girl likes to know her options.

I was inside the HVPTS before Neptune's signal ended. When Pika played with the young boy earlier, she was in typical Gremlon form. Gremlons didn't have an aggressive bone in their pale pink bodies. If Martians had cornered her, she'd be helpless. And I'd had my own run-in with Martians, enough to know playing nice wasn't a part of the communications officers' handbook.

I entered "12" into the sector designation

keypad. The seal on the transport chamber activated. I slapped my hand against a large red button on the wall. *Ka-chunk!* A burst of pressurized air launched me up through the tube toward Sector 12. I tumbled out of the chute seven seconds later.

Seven seconds too late.

Pika was in a ball on the floor. Gremlons often shrank into themselves when they were scared, and by the looks of Pika, she was nearly terrified to death. She was curled into a fetal position, her pointy ears pressed back against her head, her eyes so big they filled 80 percent of her face. Her mouth, which held fifty teeth, was drawn into a tiny little dot. Her long, gangly arms were wrapped around her knobby knees, and the Martians kicked her back and forth between them like a soccer ball.

"Leave her alone," I said.

The Martians, surprised by my sudden presence, turned their back on Pika. She rolled toward the wall, resting against the bright orange carpeting. "Hey look," said the tallest of the Martians, (which wasn't saying much since Martians are little and green by nature), "It's a piece of Plunian garbage. Forget the Gremlon. Let's take out the trash instead."

The gang of little men glared at me. Martians have large, bulbous heads, heavy brow bones, and big ears. They are glabrous too, which adds to the appearance of youth. Martians were known to be some of the scrappiest fighters in the universe simply because they'd been taken advantage of one time too many. In cases like this, they deserved a fight.

For reasons unknown to me, the green men were not in uniform. Aside from the glaring violation of departure day procedures, it made it impossible for me to know if I outranked them.

I planted my feet shoulder-width apart and braced myself for whatever they brought. In the months between voyages, I'd met a Hapkido master named Mattix Dusk who taught me the basics of self-defense in exchange for equipment repairs on his ship. The day I left for work aboard Moon Unit 6 was the day he took off for parts unknown. We'd both gotten what we wanted.

The lead Martian approached me. The HVPTS lacked oxygen, and while seven seconds wasn't long, I was short of breath. I fought to keep him from knowing that.

"What's your name, Plunian?" the Martian asked.

"Lieutenant Stryker. Who are you?"

"Bottol."

"What's your rank, Bottol?"

"Officer. Communications."

"Was that a display of your communications I just witnessed?" I asked.

"You didn't 'witness' anything. That Gremlon

doesn't belong on this ship. We were about to take a sample of her tissue to log into the database."

"Why?"

"Everybody on this ship gets printed in the database. Gremlons too."

Data-printing was the process of taking a sample of someone's tissue with a biometric device and cataloging it in the system. It wasn't a requirement of Moon Unit Corporation, so I questioned the motivation behind the Martian's desire to do it.

I kept my feet planted on the carpet. My gravity boots were more cumbersome than the sleek style favored by other members of the crew, but they expanded the surface area of my soles, which gave me better balance and traction than the standard issue footwear. I kept my eyes on Bottol while sensing the other three Martians creeping in on me.

"Pika," I said without breaking eye contact with Bottol, "Are you okay?"

"Yes," she said in a very soft voice.

"Can you stand?"

"Yes."

I grabbed a set of keys from an unsuspecting Martian and handed them to her. "Stand up and take the passenger hallways to security section. If you encounter any sealed doors, use these to get out."

"But—"

"I'll take care of the Martians. Go."

The little green men chuckled. Bottol put his hand on his space gun, while a second one held the biometric device he'd planned to use on Pika. I was legitimately on this ship, and my physiological imprint was already in the computer. There's nothing his equipment could do to me.

He spun a dial on top of the device and gray air sprayed out in a conical mist.

"You can act as tough as you want, Plunian. This hallway is sealed, and as soon as the noxious gas overcomes the oxygen content, you'll be a waste of space."

The other Martians laughed at his insult.

I didn't laugh for two reasons. The first was that he was right.

The second was that he was distracted and if I was going to take out four Martians in a hallway brawl, I needed the element of surprise.

I used a percussive hand strike and knocked the device from the Martian's hand. It landed on the carpet by where Pika had been. Bottol struck me. I grabbed his arm and pinched the pressure point on his Trapezius—the tender and vulnerable spot between his neck and his shoulder. He bent his head to the side to minimize the effect, too late. While I had him incapacitated, I launched a jump kick at another Martian, knocking him into the wall. The remaining two charged me. I bent low over my center of gravity and flipped first one and then the other over my back. The Martian I'd knocked into the wall aimed his space gun at me, and I grabbed Bottol by his shirt and held him in front of me as a shield. He took the impact and dropped back onto the carpet, unconscious.

I activated the comm device. "Martians down in Sector 12. Pika on her way to you. Lieutenant Stryker returning to uniform ward. Over."

They say bad things happen in threes. I'd been on the ship less than an hour and already had two problems under my belt. I hopped into the HVPTS and hit the button on the wall. The poor air quality had affected me, but in addition to Hapkido, Mattix had taught me breathing techniques. I watched the timer on the wall. In seven seconds, I'd be back at the uniform ward.

Four seconds. Five seconds. Six seconds. Seven seconds.

Eight seconds.

Nine seconds.

What?

The HVPTS popped open, and I fell out of the tube onto the cold, hard floor of security section. I immediately recognized the barebones design and the rudimentary equipment. And the massive mountain of muscle towering over me.

"Stryker," Neptune said. "Get up."

I rolled to my side and stared at his giant black boots. I'd get up when I was good and ready.

"That's an order from a senior officer."

I looked at him. "Are you kidding me? You, mister 'I'm so tuff I don't need a title' are going to pull rank on me?" I pushed myself to a sitting position, and then pulled myself up using the corner of his desk as leverage. "After all we've been through, you still don't trust me. I'm insulted."

I dusted imaginary security section floor dust particles off my uniform. When I looked up at Neptune, I swear I caught traces of a smile.

"Where's Pika?" I asked.

"Medi-Bay."

"Is that wise?"

"Pika has every right to be on this ship. She's on the passenger manifest. The Martians were bullying her unnecessarily. If she wanted to press charges, she could."

"How did Pika afford a ticket aboard Moon Unit 6? This trek is all anybody's talked about! Those tickets cost more than we got for a full delivery of dry ice from Plunia."

Neptune crossed his arms.

"Fine, I'll ask her." I turned to leave. Neptune put his hand on my arm above my elbow and spun me around to face him. My skin glowed bright purple, barely hiding my hot temper.

"Go to your station."

I shook his hand off and headed toward the elevators while mimicking him under my breath. "Go to your station, Stryker. Stay out of trouble, Stryker. Save your friend from Martians while I'm mingling with the captain, Stryker."

"Stryker!" Neptune called out behind me. I turned slowly. "Good work."

Huh. That was new.

THERE WAS NO POINT ARGUING WITH NEPTUNE over his command that I return to my station. It's what any ranking officer would have told me to do. We'd probably only just passed the breakaway point, and already I'd made four little green enemies. On the last moon trek, I'd only made one. I guess I like to show improvement.

The passenger elevator rose from the sub-basement and stopped on level two. The ship was designed like a giant layer cake. Neptune and the security sector were the bottom layer along with engineering and janitorial service. Various crew wards were the middle: Medi-Bay, uniforms, the vending machines, general supply, and the employee lounge. The top floor was the one the passengers had paid big bucks to experience. Spacious quarters, elaborate entertainment, and two observation decks, one on each side of the ship. The bridge was on the middle floor and OB Two overlooked it so, at designated times, passengers could watch the crew in action.

In a couple of hours, the senior level officers would be at First Dinner with the passengers and the second level crew would be in charge. Under normal circumstances, uniform lieutenant wasn't important enough of a rank to get those privileges, but the captain had personally invited me to join her at her table. Nothing was going to keep me from being at First Dinner—not my new boss's attitude, not a group of bullying Martians, not even the cart of soiled uniforms that sat in the hallway in front of the uniform ward.

Already?

I shook my head and pushed the cart, but it didn't move. I backed up and then pushed again, this time harder.

Tiny citron sparkles like the ones I'd seen during opening ceremonies floated from the other side of the cart, and the air smelled like the sugar molecules in the center of the dust cloud that surrounded the Milky Way. I backed the cart up one more time, but instead of pushing it into my ward, I circled to the front.

That's where I found the body of Xina Astryd, the winner of the publicity contest. While my stomach turned, I checked her condition with my emergency vital sign scanner and confirmed my worst fear: she was dead.

Problem number three was a doozy.

5: XINA

The Book of Protocols spelled out specific instructions for the discovery of a dead body on a Moon Unit and the first step was to remove the body from public viewing. I suspected the rule had been written with accidental—not suspicious—death in mind, but it wasn't my vast knowledge of the BOP that told me the hallway was not the place for Xina Astryd's body. It was common sense. Someone wanted me to find her, and I wasn't going to give that someone the satisfaction of seeing *what* I did *when* I did. I dragged Xina by the wrists into the uniform ward. Once she was stretched out on the carpet by the base of the cleaning machines, I called Neptune.

"What?"

"Body."

"Where?"

"Uniform ward."

"Identity?"

"The contest winner, Xina Astryd."

"Call Doc," he said. "I'm on my way."

I already knew it would take Neptune seven seconds in the HVPTS. Alerting Doc would take all seven of them. So would inspecting Xina's body to find clues.

I activated the direct radio controls on the wall. "Uniform ward to Medi-Bay. Emergency protocol requested."

"Sylvia?" said the familiar voice of Doc Edison. "Glad to have you back on the ship. You okay?"

"It's not me, Doc, it's a passenger."

"Condition?"

"Deceased." The HVPTS chute opened and Neptune dropped out, expertly landing on both feet.

"Call the security ape. Tell him I'm busy and can't spare the time attending to someone who can't benefit from my help."

Neptune's build was more gorilla than ape, but I thought it better not to correct the doc out loud. "He's already here."

"What does he have, sonic hearing? Tell him to call me when he's done. Over."

I turned back to Neptune. He was bent over the body. There was something about the way he brushed the long, cellophane strands of hair away from her face that threw me. I already knew Neptune had a reputation as a womanizer, and I knew some things about his past: he was former space military, had been tasked to teach at the academy, got caught having an affair with one of his students, and was stripped of his credentials. I knew that student was my new boss, Daila Teron. What I didn't know was how their relationship had ended or how many other women he'd been with.

He cocked his head to the side and asked in a low voice, "Where was she?"

"In the hall."

"Details?"

"On the carpet. In front of the laundry bin."

He picked up her arm and ran his fingertips over a purplish mark. I grabbed a cleaning cloth from the dispenser and dropped onto the ground next to Neptune. He pushed my hand away and I pushed back. "It's not a bruise, and it's not evidence. It's grease from the laundry cart tires."

He let go of my hand. I applied the cleaning cloth to Xina's iridescent flesh again and rubbed until the grease came off. Sparkles floated in a halo around the surface of her skin. I handed the cloth to Neptune and watched as he gently cleaned an open wound on her forehead that I hadn't noticed. That *was* evidence. And I knew Neptune knew it.

I mentally reviewed the protocol checklist. Remove the body from public zones. Report the body to Medi-Bay immediately. Isolate the body until Medi-Bay conducts tests and determines cause of death. Contain the knowledge until the risk is identified and removed.

I'd removed the body as dictated. I'd reported the body to Medi-Bay. I'd isolated the body in the uniform ward.

But Neptune wasn't waiting for Doc.

Neptune wasn't conducting tests.

And Neptune was removing evidence of Xina's cause of death.

There was a time when I'd indicated through psychological profiles that I would abide by the rules I was given. That time was in the past. I'd since learned there were times to break with proce-dure, but until Neptune let me know what was going on, I was in the dark.

"Protocol says—" I started.

He cut me off. "I know." He put his arms under Xina's head and knees and lifted her body like he was lifting a pillow. He carried her to the bench next to the inventory closet and stretched her out. "Blanket."

I pulled a fresh blanket out of plastic packaging and handed it to him. He draped it over her and held her hand.

"You have to call Doc," I said. "It's the rule."

"Doc's busy."

"He'll change his priorities."

The whole time we conversed, Neptune kept his back to me. I knew his one and two-word answers meant nothing. Neptune believed in conservancy of speech, gesture, and emotion. But his willful disregard for the rules was unexpected. Being former military, he was programmed to follow orders and eliminate threats. I'd seen this in action.

"Neptune, tell me what you want me to do. You know me. I know the rules, but I'll break them if you say so. Give me some direction."

I waited for him to say something. He didn't. His jaw clenched, and his muscles tensed.

I filled his silence with what I knew. "I know she's the winner of the publicity contest. I know that's going to look bad for Moon Unit 6. I know from the gash on her forehead that her death wasn't accidental, and I know somebody wanted me to find her in the hall outside my ward." I paused for a moment. "What I don't know is who she is to you."

Neptune bent down and tucked Xina's arm under the blanket. He raised the blanket over her face and then looked back at me.

"Xina was my sister."

6: FOLLOWING PROCEDURE

HIS SISTER? NEPTUNE DIDN'T HAVE A SISTER.
Neptune didn't have family. If you looked up the
word "loner" in the unabridged intergalactic dictio-
nary, you'd see a picture of Neptune. Yet I couldn't
deny that something about the death of the Venusian who'd won the publicity contest had affected
the man in front of me on a level I'd not yet known
possible.

Neptune stood and left the ward. I followed.
The hallway was empty. Neptune circled the
laundry cart, bent down to examine the wheels
more closely, and then stood. He pulled a recording
device off his belt and held it up. A white light
pulsed out of the recorder. Slowly, he pivoted in a
circle, capturing details of the hallway. It was standard procedure, but there wasn't anything there to
record. Aside from tire impressions in the new

carpet, there were no signs anything amiss had happened.

Neptune went back inside. I pushed the cart after him. I rolled it to the far side of the wall next to the sanitizing chambers.

"Tell Doc we need a body transported, and there's no threat of contamination," he said.

"He wanted you to call him—"

"I'll see him in person."

The questions in my head felt like an active particle field pelting the exterior of the ship. Yet as much as I wanted to ignore protocol and demand Neptune talk to me, I knew if we didn't follow procedure, we'd raise suspicion. And if what Neptune said was true, the last thing he'd want was the scrutiny that came with raised questions.

I radioed Medi-Bay. "Uniform ward to Medi-Bay. Code White. Requesting transport of body. Threat of contamination not suspected. Confidentiality requested. Over."

There was a short pause, and then, "Medi-Bay staff on its way. Over."

I was used to Neptune being the one in charge, but that didn't mean I wouldn't step up if the situation required me to do so. This situation required it.

"Give her space," I said. "Doc will need to examine Xina and you standing that close won't allow him to do so." Neptune didn't move. "Are you ready to take my report?" I asked.

He looked confused for a nanosecond and then the familiar Neptune, the unemotional, task-driven, results-oriented rule follower returned. He held his recorder toward me. "State your name and rank."

"Sylvia Stryker. Lieutenant, second class. Uniform ward."

He held the recorder closer to him. "For cataloging purposes, list the events as you recall. Use no extraneous wording."

"Upon entering crew hallway, I observed the laundry cart in front of the uniform ward. I tried to push it, but something had blocked the wheels. Examination of source revealed the body of—" I stopped talking and searched Neptune's face. His black eyes were as cold as meteorites. He nodded once, and I continued. "Xina Astryd."

"Identity confirmed by security officer Neptune."

The doors swished open, and Doc entered with a medic. Doc was everything you'd expect to get in someone who was the head of Moon Unit Medi-Bay: crotchety, ornery, and—once you got past the gruff exterior—gentle as a Tribble. As far as he was concerned, only one part of the ship's crew was essential, and that was the medical team. The rest of us were merely here to inconvenience him by getting sick, injured, and, in today's case, dead.

"Where's the victim?" he asked.

"Over here." I shot a look at Neptune. He stepped back.

Doc approached her body and lifted the blanket. "Holy smokes," he said. "That's the contest winner, isn't it?"

"Yes."

Doc examined the body and called out observations over his shoulder to the medic who stood a few feet behind him. It was fortunate that without having to eavesdrop, I heard his dictation. "Visible head wound indicates cause of death to be blunt force trauma. Venusian coloring indicates high levels of cyan in system which could indicate toxicity." He turned to me. "Good job calling the Code White. Alert Captain Ryder. In person. She's on the bridge."

"Lieutenant Stryker stays here," Neptune said. "I'll report."

"No, you won't," Doc countered. "There are at least fifty passengers in the observation booth. When you walk onto the bridge and request a private audience with the captain, they'll fear the worst. Moon Unit Corp was clear about protocol on this ship. Number one priority is public relations." Doc gestured to Xina. "This is a PR nightmare."

Neptune's hands balled into fists. I wasn't about to let the two officers get into a sparring match. Neptune was bigger, stronger, and scarier, but Doc had an immobilization device that would render Neptune unconscious in under a second.

"I'm on my way," I said. I headed toward the door.

Neptune stopped me. "Take the HVPTS."

Again? I glanced at Doc. He was busy waving a scanner over Xina's torso.

"That's an order, Stryker."

I turned away from the door and entered the HVPTS. I punched Sector 1 on the keypad, pressed the red button, and in three seconds fell in a tumble out of the chute and into a sanitary deionization chamber. After a blast of ions pelted me, a pocket door receded into the wall, and I stepped onto the bridge. As I inhaled oxygen to compensate for the poor air quality in the HVPTS, a firm hand grabbed my arm and forced me up against the wall.

7: ANATOL

From the markings on the man's uniform: single black band around his wrist, three gold bars across his epaulets, gold star and silver Moon Unit insignia pin on his collar, I ascertained that he was the chief science officer, Commander Anatol. For the duration of the trip, his job was to act as the captain's advisor.

For the next three seconds, he was to determine if I was a threat. If he thought yes, then I'd be dead.

Commander Anatol was tall and wiry. He had neatly trimmed brown hair that was parted on the side and slicked into place. His incisors were silver and pointy, an orthodontic customization that made biting lethal. One of the commander's eyes was blue, and one was gold, and together they helped him form an assessment of me. I didn't doubt for a second that he held the balance of my life in his hands.

I didn't wait for him to reach his own conclusion. "I'm Lieutenant Stryker. Uniform ward. There's a Code White which necessitates an in-person council with Captain Ryder."

"Ordered by?"

"Neptune."

"Where's Doc?"

"In the uniform ward with the body."

"Who called Code White?"

"I did."

"Using what determinations?"

"The victim was the winner of the publicity contest."

Commander Anatol released me and walked toward a computer next to us. He typed in a command. When he turned back, he smiled. "My apologies. Based on the information you just provided, it was necessary for me to restrict the view from the observation deck before proceeding with your introduction to the captain."

"But she and I—"

"Follow me." Anatol approached the captain's chair. The other crew members on the bridge ignored my presence. "Captain Ryder, the uniform lieutenant is here to make a verbal report to you."

"She is?" Captain Ryder stood up and faced

me. "Sylvia!" She followed up her greeting with a hug.

Captain Katherine Ryder was a fellow Plunian. She was the first Plunian I knew who had left our planet to attend the space academy, and after I got accepted, I read everything I could about her career path. She showed leadership qualities early on. Like me, she hadn't come from a wealthy family, and earning her education came with a signed agreement to serve in the military army corps upon graduation. When she'd completed her required four thousand hours of service, she surprised everyone by returning to the academy to teach. I'd lost track of her after dropping out.

It was her name on Moon Unit Corp publicity material that convinced me to reapply. There weren't many Plunians anymore, and with my dad serving a life sentence, I wasn't itching to reconnect. But Katherine was not only purple like me, she was also female. It was like having an older sister.

The thought reminded me of Neptune and Xina. I still couldn't make sense of that, but until we talked, I wasn't going to include that detail in my report.

Anatol seemed surprised by Katherine's affectionate greeting and my reciprocation. His eyes widened, and he cocked his head slightly. I imagined this was what specimens in a Petri dish felt like upon being examined.

"I didn't expect to see you until tonight," she said. Unlike me, she hadn't removed her bubble helmet, and her voice was on the quiet side.

"I wish I were here under happier circumstances. We have a Code White in the uniform ward."

"Who?"

"Xina Astryd. The Venusian who won the publicity contest."

"When?"

"Not long ago."

"How?"

I paused at that one. "Doc is running the necessary tests to confirm early suspicions. Until he files his report, I think—"

"How?" she asked again. There was no avoiding the question.

"Murder."

"Navigation, you're on your own. Anatol, come with us to Council Chambers."

"Council Chambers?" I repeated with trepidation.

"It's the closest soundproof room." She put her hand on my arm. "You're a highly valued member of the crew, Lieutenant. Nobody here doubts that."

She wouldn't have said that unless she knew what had happened the last time I was there.

I followed Captain Ryder and Commander Anatol off the bridge and into a room with a rectangular table and twelve chairs. Along one wall sat charging stations outfitted with individual computer tablets. If this were a sanctioned meeting, the senior level staff of the ship would each take a tablet and then a seat at the table and receive intelligence reports before making a necessary decision. But this wasn't a sanctioned meeting. It was me, the captain, and the chief science officer. And because the captain was Plunian, for once, my purple skin put me into the majority demographic.

"Lieutenant Stryker, you can speak freely here. Tell us what happened."

For the third time, I described the events that led to finding Xina's body. If I'd returned to the uniform ward via the HVPTS, I would have finished out my shift and never run across her in the hallway. Neptune had been the one who'd directed me to return via normal passageways. Did that mean something? I didn't know.

Commander Anatol listened while Captain Ryder and I conversed. He seemed satisfied with my account of the events, and I knew once he checked it against what Doc found, he'd confirm the details. If Xina had died of natural causes, this would be over. But the gash on her forehead was something else. Someone had struck her. Someone had deliberately attacked her and taken her life.

The position of the wound indicated she'd been facing her attacker. Had she caught someone doing something they shouldn't have been doing and their only defense was to eliminate the witness? Was that why she'd been killed?

"Lieutenant Stryker," Captain said. "Are you okay?"

"Yes. I was reviewing what I knew to make sure I didn't miss any details."

Anatol spoke. "It is a common human instinct to fabricate details where there are none to satisfy the holes in one's memory and create a sense of completion to a memory loop."

"I'm Plunian," I said.

"Half Plunian," he corrected. "Which means half of your biological makeup is predestined to function erroneously and emotionally."

"I have a photographic memory."

"And if you were all Plunian like our captain, I could accept your version of events as accurate. However, taking into consideration what the victim's death could mean to the company, I feel compelled to investigate."

"That's not the chief science officer's job. That's security. Neptune is already on this," I said.

"Captain Ryder," Anatol said. "I believe, based on the importance of this trip to the new owners of the company, that a second opinion is in order. The decision is yours."

Anatol's request and insistence made no sense. There was nothing science-related about Xina's death, and as soon as Anatol talked to Doc, he'd know that. But he was leveraging the needs of Moon Unit Corp to get permission to investigate on his own. I narrowed my eyes and tried to figure out his angle.

"Permission granted. Lieutenant Stryker, make yourself available to Anatol for whatever he needs. Commander, I expect a full report by Zulu Five."

Zulu time was how we told time after departure. The clock on the ship reset the moment we took off, and that was deemed Zulu Zero. Regardless of time zones, everyone on the ship adhered to Zulu time until our trek was over.

"But—" Anatol protested.

"—Zulu Five, Anatol. That's tomorrow morning. Tonight is First Dinner, and you'll be in attendance like the rest of the crew."

"Understood, Captain."

I understood too. First Dinner had granted us a temporary reprieve, but whatever Neptune could potentially be hiding was going to come to light before half of the ship had breakfast.

8: THE COVER UP

When we exited Council Chambers, the three of us went separate directions. First Dinner was in two hours, which meant I could knock off early or return to my work assignment. This being the first day of the trek and me being an over-achiever, I returned to the uniform ward, unsure of who or what I'd find when I arrived.

I took the secret stairs. There were no signs that Neptune, Xina, or Doc and his crew had ever been there. The sparkly tendrils that surrounded Xina earlier were gone. The laundry bin was gone. The uniform ward looked exactly as it had when I first took my post.

The last direct order I'd received from my immediate boss had been to learn the BOP. If Daila showed up and gave me a pop quiz, I'd pass easily.

Tomorrow small jobs would trickle in, but today, nothing.

I should have knocked off early.

I logged my work hours into the ledger and opened the uniform closet to get my helmet and oxygen. A thick black identification card fell from the shelf and landed by the toe of my gravity boot. The ID had my picture on it and the credentials MOON UNIT 6 SECURITY.

I knew who was responsible. I just didn't know why.

I was unclear on how the comm device worked, but so far it seemed like Neptune responded when I spoke. "Does this ID card mean what I think it means?" I asked, half to myself and half to him.

"It means you're on my staff," he answered.

I wondered if I'd ever get used to having another voice in my head. "I'm on uniform duty. Officially and legitimately. And everybody on this ship knows it."

"That's your cover. Meet me in your chambers in twenty minutes."

"*In* my chambers? Don't you mean *in front of* my chambers? Because I *know* you're not planning on going into my room when I'm not there."

There was no answer.

I stuck the ID card into my pocket and locked up. Crew quarters were just past the employee cafeteria. The noise level inside indicated that more than one non-ranking officer had taken advantage of the light workload today to enjoy a shortened shift. I strode past the camaraderie and into my corridor.

Neptune was in the hallway. A small victory! I deactivated the door security measures. He entered before me. Victory defeated.

My quarters on Moon Unit 6 were slightly larger than the last time, for no reason other than the luck of the draw. My bed was folded up along the far wall, and a dresser sat next to it. A few feet from the foot of the bed was a tall closet that held my personal items, still packed. My bag required my thumbprint to deactivate the locks. The ship stewards were responsible for distributing our belongings to our respective quarters, but the unpacking process was up to me. Not that that would take long. Outside of what I'd brought onto this ship in my compact bag, I had nothing.

I pulled the ID card from my pocket and held it out to Neptune. "Take it back. I don't want you to give me a job because you think I'll keep your secret. When I become a Moon Unit security officer, it'll be because I earned it. The hard way."

"I can't trust anyone else."

"You're using my dreams of working in security as a bribe."

"Those credentials were waiting for you all along. It's not my fault you applied for the wrong job."

I studied his face. Neptune was, by most accounts, unreadable. He was a tall, broad-shouldered, muscular with tawny skin, hands double the size of mine, and a neck thicker than my thigh. The lines and planes of his face were like features etched into moon rock. Unflinching. Unemotional. Unreadable.

Neptune was the protector of everybody. That's why he made such a good security officer. And he'd been given the job by a friend who knew what he was capable of—a plan that had backfired for at least one party involved. The night I learned that my planet had been destroyed, Neptune had protected me in a way I'd never experienced. He'd treated me as an equal. He'd put his life on the line for me, but why? I was nobody to him. I was just a crew member on the ship.

But as he stood facing me, waiting for me to respond to his words, a thought entered my mind. If Neptune protected everybody, then who protected Neptune?

"What do you need me to do?" I asked.

"Cover up Xina's real identity."

"But she won the publicity contest. You said every finalist was cleared for travel beforehand so there wouldn't be any problem when Moon Unit Corp announced the winner. And you told me she worked on Colony 7 in the entertainment industry."

"Xina didn't win that contest legitimately. She didn't work in the entertainment industry. That was a cover story. I rigged the results to guarantee her spot on the ship. I uploaded her data, falsified her medical charts, and entered the keywords Moon Unit Corp was looking for in a winner. I hired a computer expert to alter the randomizer so that it would select her name." If he hadn't provided such detail, I wouldn't have believed him.

"I don't get it. If you wanted Xina on the ship so badly, you could have arranged it. You're a senior officer." I waved the ID card. "You can produce credentials at the drop of a gravity boot. Why not just make her part of your crew? Or assign her another position on the ship?"

"Xina never would have passed the medical exam."

"Those medical exams are inaccurate, and you know it. *I* didn't pass the medical exams for our last trip, and I was fine. I was better than fine."

"Xina wasn't fine. She was dying. Her final wish was to die on Venus and the only way I knew to guarantee that was to get her on board this ship."

What Neptune didn't say, what I didn't say,

what we both had to be thinking, was that she would have died anyway. Which meant someone else on this ship knew of her condition and wanted to make sure she didn't reach her destination. Now I had two questions: who, and why.

9: SECRETS AND LIES

"Doc already ran Xina's vital signs," I said. "When he feeds the recording into his database, he's going to get a diagnosis."

"I'll make sure Doc has other priorities," Neptune said.

"—And Captain Ryder told Commander Anatol to give her a full report on Xina's murder by Zulu Five."

"That's going to cause a problem. We need a plan, and we don't have much time."

"Hold up," I said. "Tonight is First Dinner. You're expected to be there."

"You're not."

"Yes, I am."

Neptune's eyebrows dropped down over his eyes, and three vertical lines appeared between them. "Who invited you?"

"Captain Ryder asked me to join her at her table."

Neptune's face relaxed, and he stood up. "Then we'll have less time than I thought. Choose your First Dinner outfit carefully. We're going on a mission after dessert." He stormed out.

Leave it to Neptune to trump the idea of attending First Dinner as a guest of the captain with the one thing I'd want more. To be deployed on a secret mission on board the ship. I guess I was weird that way.

I stripped down to my purple skin and stepped into the deionization chamber to freshen up, setting the finishing spray on luminescent. Just because I was going on a security mission later didn't mean I couldn't doll up a little first. While the spray bonded with my skin, I opened the closet and pulled out my luggage. After deactivating the lock, I rooted underneath a few spare uniforms and found my silver space panties. I dressed in leggings made from Stealthyester®, a patented stretch fabric that took on transformative color properties and served as a second skin. I added a form-fitting, rubberized top with removable sleeves.

The only nice garment I had that would hide the durable gear was a multi-layer white dress that swept the floor. I stuffed the rubberized top's sleeves into a deceptively small silver pouch that clipped onto the side of my dress, added a lipstick and an inhaler filled with oxygen charges, and left.

First Dinner was in the Space Bar on the top level of the ship. I wanted to experience every single benefit that came from being the captain's guest, so I took the elevator all the way to the top deck and then walked through the passenger corridors alone.

A very tall and very thin Venusian couple walked past me, holding hands. The man wore a metallic paisley tunic over matching pants. The woman had long, straight white hair, parted in the center, and wore a flowing silver lamé gown. They smiled politely. A trail of sparkly dust and the sweet scent of sugar fluttered in their wake, though the speed at which they moved indicated they were in no hurry to reach their destination.

Hmmm. That made three Venusians on the ship. You'd think the novelty of their planet would have worn off by now.

The small boy who'd been chasing Pika around OB One ran ahead of a man and woman dressed in what must have passed for evening attire on Earth. In contrast to the crew's mandatory white attire for First Dinner, the guests in black tie stood out like sore thumbs.

Medical advances had prolonged the lifespan of people from Earth, and the resulting overpopulation of the third planet from the sun had driven scientists to find ways to make other planets livable. Somewhere in the late twenty-first century, they'd taken what they learned from decades of space exploration and colonized Mars. Shortly after, they branched out to other planets, making galactic relocation a thing. But that was way in the past. And these days, nobody thought all that much about it.

The mines on Plunia were widely credited with changing the state of several planets to habitable thanks to the time-release nature of dry ice. My family had owned the largest and most reliable mines in the galaxy and was highly respected— until my dad was caught doing business with pirates and restricting the supply of dry ice to drive prices higher.

The name Jack Stryker used to mean something, and I'd been proud to be his daughter. Now the Stryker name was a joke. I'd spent years of my life studying, training, working hard, and sticking to the rules to prove I wasn't like him. But no matter what I did, people heard my name and assumed I was an ice chip off the old block. Jack Stryker could rot in jail on Colony 13 with the other criminals for all I cared. His actions had destroyed my family, and the space pirates had destroyed our planet. If I were a minor, I'd be a homeless ward of the state. Lucky me, I was a legal adult, which classified me as a bum instead.

After the last moon trek, the Moon Unit

owners had arranged for passengers and crew to be dropped off either at home or at temporary housing at the academy. Neptune extended an offer for me to live on his land. But as much as I appreciated Neptune saving my life, I had other priorities. I chose the academy. Not to get my degree, but to use their information database. I wanted to learn everything I could about space pirates because the first chance I got, I was going to design a mission to make them pay for what they'd done. Revenge wasn't smart or sweet, but I couldn't let them get away with their acts of destruction.

During my research, I discovered that Federation Council, the governing body of the galaxy, had captured the pirate Cheung Qidd. They held him in solitary confinement with a life sentence. He was never going to see a day of freedom again in his life, so it had been up to him whether he wanted to uphold the pirate code. He did. At least, he did for the first 71,186 hours he spent there. In hour 71,187, he requested counsel.

Cheung Qidd was sick and wanted to unburden himself before he died. Federation Council arranged private sessions with a high-ranking member of the military who recorded every secret Qidd shared. The transcripts were lengthy, classified, and encrypted. I hired my friend Zeke Champion to decipher them for me, but the only information he was able to strip out of the documents were names. Of the thousands of names mentioned, two stood out: Jack Stryker and Neptune.

Neptune knew my dad. Something he'd never told me, never mentioned, never held over my head, never shared. Whatever it was he knew, it was intel that came after my father was arrested. I had a right to know, and by never mentioning it, he chose a side. It wasn't mine.

And now that the tables were turned, I didn't know how that would affect me. Neptune's sister had been murdered on this ship, and the only reason she was here was because he'd broken protocol and gotten her onto the passenger manifest. If I wanted to, I could go directly to the captain and report him. I could have him taken into custody and moved to a cell on Colony 13 with my dad. I could talk to my ex-boyfriend, Vaan Marshall, the youngest member of Federation Council, who'd been collecting evidence against Neptune since the last moon trek. I could choose a side too.

If I were the soldier I'd hoped to become by attending the academy, that's what I would have done. But I didn't. I couldn't. Because the only way to learn what Neptune knew about my dad was to work with him—for now.

10: ON ASSIGNMENT

I ARRIVED AT THE SPACE BAR, AND A MEMBER of the restaurant staff escorted me to the captain's table. It was at the front of the room, the center of attention, by the stage. All eyes were on me. Before sitting, I glanced around. The Martians that had bullied Pika in Sector 12 were at a table along the back wall. Ofra Starr was in a white velvet wrap jacket and matching white trousers. Small white and silver lightning bolts had been painted on his cheekbones. My boss sat with a clean-cut man with shiny black hair. Figured she'd be buttering up TJ Woodward, the ship's personnel director. He smiled and waved while she scowled, apparently not happy that I was at the captain's table and she was not.

I did not see Neptune.

"Lieutenant Stryker, welcome to First Dinner,"

Captain Ryder said. She'd changed into her dress white uniform but still wore her helmet. "Have a seat next to Officer Lumiere."

I'd been so busy scanning the room that I'd failed to recognize the Independent Border Patrol officer at our table. I smiled and lowered myself into the vacant seat next to him. "Officer Lumiere, I didn't expect to see you tonight."

"You two know each other?" Captain Ryder asked.

"We met on OB One." I turned to him. "Border Patrol sounds like fascinating work. Is there a reason your job brought you on the trek to Venus, or were you able to parlay an assignment into a getaway?"

"I prefer not to talk about my work," Lumiere said. "I'd rather talk about you."

It was going to be a long dinner.

Nyota Zuni, the Space Bar hostess, stopped by our table. Her white dress was a sleeveless column with a high slit over one thigh, revealing silver sandals that laced up her calves to her knee. She greeted Captain Ryder and her guests, perfect timing as far as I was concerned. In addition to the captain, IBP, and me, the other guests at the table were the couple dressed in black with the small boy who had chased Pika the day of departure.

From the round of introductions, I learned their names. Yesenia, George, and the young boy,

Ellison. George had his hands full with Ellison. Yesenia watched and smiled but left the job of managing the boy to his dad. I secretly diagnosed Ellison as having an untreated attention deficit disorder. He slid down under the tablecloth. His father reprimanded him, he returned to his seat, and he did it again. The third time, George called Nyota to our table and whispered something in her ear. She left and returned with a portable chair with a seatbelt. Ellison was instructed to sit in the chair. Problem solved, though not without a fair amount of embarrassment on the sides of many of the parties involved.

Small talk lapsed as plates of Plutonian pasta were served alongside glasses of richly pigmented Saturnian wine. I ate everything that came my way. As of tomorrow, it was the crew cafeteria vending machines for a protein mix for me. We finished with flavored balls of ice replicated in a lab. The display was pleasing: clear crystal bowls of pink, purple, and green, but having grown up with pure Plunian ice, I could taste the difference. I caught the captain's eyes, and she winked at me. Apparently, I wasn't the only ice snob on the ship.

As the laboratory ice balls disappeared, I grew antsy. Neptune expected me to join him, but he'd said nothing about how to get away or where to meet him. The lights dimmed, and Nyota took the stage to welcome everyone to First Dinner. I glanced at my tablemates, noting the men seemed more interested in the slit in her dress than her greeting. She introduced the two tall and narrow Venusians that I'd passed in the hallway as Synn and Shyrr. A halo of sparkly shimmer followed them onto the stage and hung in a cloud around each of their heads. It turned out they were the entertainment.

I relaxed. Maybe Neptune changed his mind. Maybe he'd reconsidered asking me to give up my coveted position at the captain's table to do something that could get me kicked off the ship. Maybe he had come to his senses.

The Venusian vocalists' voices were hypnotic. I closed my eyes to fully appreciate the music. Something struck the front of my dress. I looked down and saw a mint green stain on my left boob. Across the table, Ellison grinned. I assessed the table for a clean napkin or glass of water, but there were neither.

"Stryker," said a voice in my head. "Pay attention." I sat up in my chair. Where was he? "Create a diversion and meet me in security. Use the HVPTS."

I couldn't argue, and Neptune knew it. But I'd taken the High Pressure Velocity Transport System too many times today and was feeling the effects. Rapid transport was for emergencies for that reason. Nobody expected a person to have three legitimate emergencies in one day. My internal rhythms were off, and after the last trip, I felt lightheaded.

"Do you copy?" he asked.

I shook my head from side to side.

"You don't copy, or you aren't going to take the HVPTS?"

I raised my hand to my face and pressed two fingers against my temple.

"Fine. Excuse yourself from the table and leave. I'll start without you."

I tucked the first of my two fingers into my palm, leaving only my middle finger pressed against my face. I'd picked up all sorts of ways to communicate in language class.

"Non-verbal communication received."

Neptune's direction had changed from creating a diversion and taking the HVPTS to excusing myself early and meeting him. Option 1 would get me to him in under two minutes. Option 2 would take upward of ten. That meant eight minutes where Neptune would work on his own, unsupervised, on a non-sanctioned, secret mission.

Maybe I'd never attend First Dinner again, but frankly, these Venusians were putting the crowd to sleep, and that seemed like the opposite of what I needed.

I scanned the faces of my tablemates. Their attention was fully focused on the floor show, except for Ellison in his chair, who held a spoon like a catapult aimed my direction. I looked down at my dress and, with disgust, saw that the lime green stain had spread. My best dress. The little jerk.

I got an idea. I knew exactly how to create a diversion.

I put my hand on Lumiere's arm and leaned close. "Excuse me, Officer, don't you think Ellison deserves to be untethered for the duration of the evening? He's been very well behaved." Lumiere looked from me to George and Yesenia, who had their eyes closed. "I think his parents have entered a Venusian-triggered trance," I added.

The border patrol agent turned to Ellison and released his seatbelt. Immediately the boy slid down from his seat and disappeared under the table like before. This time, he made his way under the cloth, out the other side, and all the way to the stage before being noticed. He reached out and touched the ankle of Shyrr. Her vocal emissions were interrupted with an off-key yell. Synn tried to cover up with a basso profundo, which lulled the audience back into their musical stupor.

"I'll handle this." I jumped up from my seat, snatched Ellison from the base of the stage, and carried him to the kitchen where I handed him to Nyota.

"Thank you," she said. "That could have been a disaster."

"Keep him occupied back here until the Venusians are done with their act." I ran my hands along the wall in search of the security door.

"What do you think you're doing?" she demanded. Her tone seemed slightly less appreciative than before.

Slowly I turned around and pointed at the lime green stain on my boob. "I can't go back to the captain's table like this. Can you point me toward the employee exit?"

11: NEPTUNE'S MISSION

I STRIPPED IN THE HALLWAY ON THE WAY TO the HVPTS. By the time I entered the travel chamber, I was in my Stealthyester® leggings and rubber top. The surface of the fabric reflected my surroundings and helped me blend in. I removed the sleeves from my pouch and pulled them on too. A gap of purple skin showed by each of my shoulders, but I was otherwise protected. I shook the residual haze of Venusian Trance from my brain and typed Sector X into the keypad. (The "X" was achieved by pressing the odd numbers in this order: 1-5-9-3-5-7. Security section was classified and not included in the general info that had been released to the public. To anyone not in the know or privy to information acquired through back channels, it didn't exist.)

I landed on the cold concrete floor in a tumble,

rolled, and stood. The forward momentum left me dizzy. I fell into Neptune's firm, broad chest. He put his hands on my upper arms and steadied me. My balance returned, and I stepped away. "What's the mission?" I asked. He said nothing. "Come on, Neptune, we don't have a ton of time. I'm ready for a mission, but I can't act if I don't know your plan."

He turned to the side and spoke. I could see his face in profile. "We have to delete Xina's medical panel from Doc's computer."

"You can't do that," I said. "As soon as Doc sees her medical panel is gone, he'll know someone tampered with the information. He'll open an investigation, and it'll create all sorts of problems. You know this."

"Doc cannot analyze her tissue. I'll take my chances."

"You're too close to the situation. Let me design the mission."

"No time." Neptune stormed away. I followed. He wasn't being honest with me, but I didn't yet know why. The only thing I knew was that this was so important to him that he'd risk his position for it. Considering I was in on his plan, my position with Moon Unit Corporation was slightly tenuous as well.

We reached the dark gray master computer that sat outside the holding cell. Neptune dropped into the chair and activated the dark network. The screen went black, and then ten white squares popped up on the screen. He entered his password and the blank screen was replaced with a series of pop-up windows that flashed News, Diagnostics, Passenger Files, Encrypted Data.

Neptune had no idea how smart he'd been to include me in his mission. "Get up," I said.

"No."

"Get up!" I grabbed his shoulder and leaned back, pulling him (or trying to) out of his chair. The chair spun around, and he was face to face with my rubber boobs. I took advantage of his temporary distraction to tip the hydraulic chair forward, and he fell out. I sat down, spun toward the screen, and typed a string of characters that, to the untrained eye would appear to be gibberish, into the command menu.

"Stryker."

"Not now, Neptune. Xina's files are going to be under Encrypted Data, and there's no way you or I are going to crack those files in the next seven hours. We need help."

"No."

I whirled back around. "Yes. You can't do this by yourself. I know you know that because you asked me to help you. You said you trust me. So, trust me."

His eyes bored holes into me. We wasted precious seconds in a stare-off. I did not look away.

The computer beeped with an incoming message. I spun around and read the screen.

>>WHAT DO YOU NEED?

"Who is that?"

"A friend of mine from the academy."

"I need a name."

"Zeke Champion."

Neptune lost only a second more. "Go."

I typed. *Need to access encrypted data on Moon Unit 6*

>>AND HERE I THOUGHT YOU WERE GOING TO ASK FOR SOMETHING HARD

It's important, I added.

>>IMPLIED BY REQUEST

Can you do it?

>>WHEN?

Now.

>>WHERE ARE YOU? NEED COMP SERIAL NUMBER

I looked at Neptune. Zeke could do what we needed him to do faster than anyone else, but by giving him the serial number of the computer, he'd have unrestricted access to everything. It was Neptune's call.

"Can he do it?" Neptune asked.

Zeke Champion had been my study partner at the space academy. When we finished out our classes on tactical advantage, we had the choice of studying either computers or drone technology. I'd opted for computers. Zeke's dad was in charge of computer repairs for space fleet vessels and wanted to learn something new. He could already out-program anybody in the galaxy.

"Yes, he can do it."

"Move."

I rolled the chair to the side, and Neptune typed in a string of fourteen characters.

>>THX. YOU OWE ME MORE THAN DINNER FOR THIS

A few seconds later came: >>I'M IN. WHICH FILE?

Neptune remained at the keyboard. *Xina Astryd.*

>>PASSENGER FILE, MEDICAL FILE, BACKGROUND FILE, OR SEALED CRIM-INAL RECORD?

The cursor blinked, waiting for the answer to the question. It appeared Neptune had withheld a few details.

12: FAMILY

I pushed Neptune out of the way. *Need to talk. Highly confidential.*

>>I'LL HACK INTO YOUR SECURITY COMM DEVICE

"How does he know about the comm device?" Neptune asked. For the first time since I'd met him, I detected genuine surprise in his voice.

"Go," I said.

Zeke's familiar and laid-back voice entered my ear. "Sylvia! How the heck are ya?"

"We can catch up later. I'm on Moon Unit 6, and there's been a murder."

"Xina Astryd. I saw her files. You know her?"

"Not really, but here's the problem. We can't let anybody see those files."

"It shouldn't matter now," he said. "Oh. Wait. Did anybody know she was terminal?"

"I don't know." Zeke now knew as much, if not more, than I did about Xina.

"Got it. The new owners of Moon Unit Corp plunked a ton of money into the publicity surrounding that trip, and you're worried about the PR nightmare when it gets out that proper health screening protocols weren't followed. How about I upload some junk Venusian DNA onto her profile? Murder is murder, so your doc can focus on why she was killed instead of what she had. Nobody has to know she was sick."

I repeated Zeke's solution to Neptune.

"Will that work?" Neptune asked.

"Who's that?" Zeke asked.

"It's Neptune."

"The scary dude you told me about?"

"Not now, Zeke." I glanced at Neptune. He was in his familiar feet-shoulder-width-apart, arms-crossed stance. His brows were lower than usual. "You can trust him. I told him he could trust you. How long will it take?"

"I need time to find a reasonable DNA match in the database and time to recode it to match your friend. Time to upload, run error checks, wipe digital fingerprints—"

"How long, Zeke?"

"Give me twelve minutes."

"Radio silence for twelve minutes."

A timer appeared in white digital numbers on

the black computer screen and started counting down. Zeke had two speeds: on the job and chatty. Now that he had an assignment and a timeframe, he was on the job. I wouldn't hear anything from the comm device or the dark network until he was finished.

Zeke's suggested solution would provide easy answers for the medical panels Doc would run. And like he'd said, with no red flags on Xina's history, Doc would be left to focus on how she died: fatal head wound. There wasn't a living being who didn't know a strike to the head could prove fatal. What we didn't know was whether that had been someone's intended goal or an accident. I doubted Neptune cared much about which motivation had killed his sister—only about the identity of who had.

That put me in a tricky position. Aside from Neptune, I was the only one who knew the truth about Xina. I knew what Zeke was doing. I was aware of at least ten different protocols we will have broken by the end of the evening if everything went as planned, which made me the only person who could testify against Neptune if any of this came to light.

That was a lot of trust for Neptune to place in me.

As the timer ticked down the seconds, I studied him. Not being able to access his computer was like putting him in a holding cell. He was predetermined to action. But for the next nine and a half minutes, he couldn't do anything but wait.

I'd never seen Neptune wait. Normally he handled issues as they arose. I didn't know what he did to unwind. Or *if* he unwound.

On our last moon trek, he'd managed a dead body, headed off sabotage of engineering, thwarted the efforts to destroy the ship, and saved my life (more than once). The whole reason he was on the staff of a Moon Unit was because he'd been stripped of his military rank and title. Jobs for someone with Neptune's qualifications and experience didn't exist in the help wanted ads. If any other opportunity had been available, he would have turned down the Moon Unit job in a heartbeat. Based on what I saw, Neptune would have self-destructed if left to his own devices. He was smart enough to see that heading security on a cruise ship was better than nothing.

At least that was my assessment. I'd spent some time on a deep dive into his background thanks to Zeke's loan of the override password to Federation Council's mainframe. But there'd been nothing about a sibling, Venusian or not. Federation Council knew everything about everything. If they didn't know about Neptune's sister, then he'd already found a way to sanitize her files (and his).

Which meant Neptune had his own way into Federation Council computers.

"Tell me about your sister," I said.

"No."

"I've never seen you stand still for more than ten minutes, and twelve minutes is two more than ten. Zeke's going to do what we asked, but you need a distraction while he does it. So, tell me about Xina."

He was quiet for a few seconds, and I thought he was possibly considering whether I'd be more or less "helpful" if placed in the temporary holding cell. (Less. I did not like spending time in holding!)

"She's younger than me. She was—" he cut himself off and stared at a spot on the floor. "She was born in a lab on Venus. Soldiers were recruited to take part in a science experiment on cross-breeding. The offspring were chipped at birth, so they could be monitored for the rest of their lives."

Chipping referred to the process of injecting a microchip subcutaneously at the base of the skull. The embedded chip would allow Federation Council to remotely monitor location, activity, and health. When someone was chipped, they lost their rights to privacy. I knew the procedure was used to track known criminals, but I'd never heard about a government project to chip cross-bred intergalactic babies for study. I wasn't exactly in the know when it came to stuff like that.

"What you're describing goes against every-thing Federation Council stands for. Those chips allow people to be monitored. If they can track Xina, then what Zeke's doing won't hide anything."

Neptune glanced at the screen, and I followed his stare. Three minutes, twelve seconds.

"Xina's mother was a Venusian who had an affair with my father," Neptune continued. "A normal, hormones-and-passion affair. Have you ever been to Venus?" I shook my head. "Met a Venusian?" I shook my head again. "They have a sort of pull. Like an undertow. When Venus is present, priorities shift."

"You're being vague."

"The sperm donors were the highest level, strong-willed soldiers out there. My dad wasn't part of the experiment. He worked at the factory. He and Xina's mother had an affair, and she became pregnant. They passed off the pregnancy as part of the study until Xina was born. My dad kidnapped her from the lab before the doctors could discover she wasn't like the others. He took her back to our home and raised her himself. I left for military training when she was ten."

It was a tragic story with elements of attraction, hope, love, and passion, things I'd never expected to be a part of Neptune's past. But there was more to the story, and we both knew it. Xina's loyalties could have shifted. She could have had ulterior motives for tracking down her big brother and asking him to pull strings to get her back to Venus. If Neptune was right about the influence Venusians had, Xina could have known about her power and used it for personal gain. And with the suggestion of a sealed criminal record, I wondered if her illness was real or if that had been part of a story designed to manipulate him into breaking the rules.

"How did she find you?" I asked. He narrowed his eyes as if assessing what I really meant to ask. "You don't exactly have a mailing address. I'm just curious."

"She didn't find me. I found her."

But before I could launch into the four thousand, eight hundred, and ninety-six questions that popped into my head, the timer went off.

13: NEXT VICTIM

"Zeke?" I said. "Are you done?"

No voice answered on the comm device. My fingers flew over the keyboard. *Request Status Report Immediately.*

>>ALMOST DONE.

>>HAD TO INTERRUPT MISSION

>>FOUND OTHER PARTY ACCESSING SAME FILES

>>OVERRIDING WOULD EXPOSE US

>>

>>

>>

>>DONE.

Access my comm device.

"What a rush!" Zeke said in my ear. "There I was, in your network, taking care of business, and then whammo! You didn't tell me I'd have competition."

"I didn't know you'd have competition."

Neptune's voice sounded in my comm device. Looked like there was a way for two people to patch into my ear at once. Since he was next to me, it was like Neptune in stereo. "Report."

And then, suddenly, there was a three-way conversation in my head.

"Oh, hey, you're that Neptune dude, right? Don't worry. Problem solved. I uploaded the medical stuff first so anybody who looks at Xina's panel is going to see your normal, everyday Venusian. Which, let's face it, isn't normal or every day, especially in Xina's case because she was a babe! No offense, Sylvia."

"None taken." There was very little in the galaxy more exotic than a sparkly Venusian woman. Even I knew that. I didn't turn around to see Neptune's expression. I could imagine it just fine, and that was bad enough.

"Anyway, you're in the clear," Zeke said.

This time I glanced at Neptune's face. "You're sure?" I asked Zeke.

"As soon as I saw someone else mucking about in the data stream I deleted the files from the network. If you didn't tell me someone else was going after her info, then maybe you didn't know. And on the off chance it wasn't her medical info they wanted, I figured you might want to be the one to decide who sees what."

"Thanks, Zeke. I owe you one."

"After the way you warmed my bed for the past three months, I'd say we're even."

I felt my skin flush. Never mind the bed warming Zeke referred to was the way I'd rewired some of his busted drones to hold a heat charge. We'd warmed them with lasers and then placed them between our blankets (on separate beds) to make the beds cozy. But Zeke was naturally flirtatious, and he'd taken to teasing me about the way I spoke of Neptune. Neptune didn't need to know the truth. It wasn't like he cared about things like that.

"Champion," Neptune barked.

"Right here," Zeke answered.

"This mission was off the books. Any related intel or residual impact from your work comes to me or Lieutenant Stryker. Whoever was on the network was violating Moon Unit protocol and may be dangerous. I'll protect your identity."

"No biggie," Zeke said. "I'm not afraid of them."

"Who?" I asked. My skin tingled with excitement. Of course, Zeke already knew who was poking around in Xina's file! This case was going to solve itself, and I would go back to being the captain's friend and working my way up the ladder of authority in the corporation.

"The Martians," Zeke said. "That's what this is about, right? Those little green men are the worst when it comes to collecting information for their database. Somebody needs to tell them the passenger lists are off-limit."

This time I did more than glance at Neptune, mostly to see if he was as surprised as I was to learn the same men who'd bullied Pika in Sector 12 were scavenging information on the dark network.

From the look on his face, he was.

We terminated communication with Zeke and left security section. Neptune went to patrol the ship and I headed to my quarters. It was Zulu One, only four hours from when Anatol was expected to deliver his report about Xina to Captain Ryder. It had been close, but thanks to Zeke's help, we dodged a bullet. I suspected Neptune's security patrol would include special attention to the Martian quadrant, but I didn't ask. It had been a long first day and the morning would come all too quickly. I changed from my Stealthyester® leggings and rubber top into a lavender sleepsuit, adjusted the temperature on my thermal blanket, and dozed off before my head hit the pillow.

I woke in midair.

I'd been so tired that I forgot to turn on the gravity pulse, and without my boots and uniform, there was nothing to hold me down on my cot. Simply put, I'd floated a couple of feet above my bed.

It wasn't the floating that jarred me awake, it was something Zeke had said. Something about Xina's files. He said he uploaded junk DNA so anybody who looked at her file would see your normal, everyday Venusian, but from what Neptune had told me, Xina wasn't your normal, everyday Venusian. She was the daughter of a Venusian and whatever Neptune's dad was, which, judging from Neptune, was human alpha male. I wasn't anywhere close to figuring out who had killed Xina or why, but if the killer knew of her relation to Neptune, they'd easily identify the mismatch. Zeke's efficiency would simply create more questions.

I reached for my pillow, floating next to me, and lobbed it at the gravity button. Upon contact, the gravity field slowly increased, and I floated down to the bed. It was Zulu Three. I'd gotten only two hours of sleep, which was going to have to be enough.

"Neptune," I said. "Are you awake?"

"I don't sleep."

Of course, he didn't. "We're going to have a problem with Xina's file."

"I'm turning off your comm device. Meet me in security section. Over."

Well, that was just great. I was going to have to change out of my sleepsuit and into a uniform. That meant there would be no going back to bed. What was the point of having Neptune's voice in my head all the time if I had to communicate with him face to face? I hated inefficiency.

I changed into my day two regulation lieutenant uniform, an orange shift with silver trim over a white turtleneck and silver gravity boots. Even if Neptune expected me there quickly, I wasn't taking the HVPTS. I still felt scrambled and dizzy from all the high-velocity transport yesterday. I reached the end of the hallway, turned right, and entered the stairwell that led to the passenger floor. Halfway up the staircase, I smelled the sweet scent of sugar. And despite the darkness, I detected sparkly tendrils of mist that curled into the air from somewhere in front of me.

I wasn't alone in the hallway. A Venusian lay face down by the stairs. I dropped onto the carpet to determine what I could about identity and vital signs of the victim. I eased the iridescent hood off the Venusian's head and discovered things were worse than I could have imagined. It wasn't a Venusian at all.

It was Pika.

14: MISTAKEN IDENTITY

THE WAIFISH PINK GREMLON WAS ALIVE BUT
out cold. I slipped my arms under her head and
knees and lifted her. "Neptune," I said. There was
no answer. "Neptune, I'm in the stairwell by Sector
4. Pika's hurt." There was no answer. "I'm taking
her to the uniform ward via the HVPTS."

Darn it! I burst through the exit and went
straight to the HVPTS tube. It wasn't built for
more than one passenger, but Pika was tiny and
together, we fit. I stood her up as best as I could and
held her with one arm, jabbing at the red button
with my elbow. When I connected, the pressure
shot us straightaway to the uniform ward. We both
tumbled out, me landing at Neptune's feet, Pika in
an unconscious ball that rolled a few feet away.

"Where was she?" he asked.

"In the stairwell by Sector 4 just past the passenger doors."

"She's alive."

"Yes."

Neptune unfastened the Venusian cape around Pika's neck, and the fabric fell to the ground. He carried her to the bench where he'd laid out Xina. "She's cold. Rub her hands. I'll rub her feet."

I did as he said. Pika twitched once, then twice, then shook her head and tried to sit up. She opened her mouth and burped, and a tendril of sparkles and glitter floated out. She drew her lips tight over her numerous teeth and clamped a hand over her mouth as if to keep more sparkles from coming out, but those that floated around her head were incriminating enough. Her eyes widened, and her small pink ears lay flat against her head.

"Pika, what's going on?" I asked. Neptune glowered at me. I glowered back. The poor pink Gremlon had already had a bad start to her trip. No matter what she'd done, right now she didn't need a lecture.

"I was lonely in my room," she said. Her lips pulled together in a pout, "so I went out into the ship. But I saw those green meanies, and I got scared. I hid in the Venusian's room until they were gone."

"Green meanies...you mean the Martians?"

She nodded. She drew her shoulders up in a

tiny hunch. "Venusians are beautiful. I knew if the Martians thought I was one of them, they'd leave me alone."

The Martians. Again. Those little green men were turning out to be more trouble than they were worth.

"You're just as beautiful as a Venusian," I told her. "But you're going to have to take the cape back to the room where you found it. Synn and Shyrr are the entertainment, and this is one of their costumes. Shyrr will probably report it missing when she realizes it's gone."

"Mine, mine, mine," Pika said. She clutched the sparkly cape to her narrow pink body.

Neptune stepped closer. "Pika, you don't have to lie."

"She's not lying," I said. I kept my eyes on Pika. "You didn't take this from Shyrr's room, did you?"

Slowly, she shook her pale head from side to side. Her body mass shrunk by about 15 percent.

"Don't be scared," I said. "Neptune and I are your friends. We're going to make sure you're okay. But I need you to answer a question first. Can you do that?"

She nodded.

"Where did you get this cape?"

"It's mine, mine, mine. Neptune's sister gave it to me."

I was shocked. Pika knew of the secret relationship between Neptune and Xina—the one he'd made such a big deal of confessing to me after I found her body? What else did Pika know? And *how* did she know? And why was Neptune okay with a Gremlon, the flibbertigibbets of the galaxy, knowing such a big secret?

"Pika," Neptune said. "I don't have a sister." Denial. Yeah, that's reliable.

"Yes, you do," Pika said. "The sparkly woman who won the contest. She came to visit you once when you weren't at home. She told me you were her big brother and she asked me all kinds of questions about you."

That didn't fit with what Neptune had told me about seeking out his sister during our three-month hiatus. I was more interested in the differences in their stories than the fact that one of them had a reason to lie.

"When did Xina give this cape to you?" I asked.

"She said I could take whatever I wanted from her room. That means it's mine."

"No, that means she let you borrow it," I said. "How did you get it from Xina's quarters? After what happened, they should either be restricted or sealed."

"I didn't take it from her room. I told you, she gave it to me. She gave me all kinds of stuff. We're friends." She turned her attention from me to

Neptune. "We are," she said again as if repeating the declaration would make us believe her.

Neptune stood up. "Stryker, a word." He moved to the door. I followed him. "Talk to her. Find out what she knows. I have a bad feeling about this, but Pika's scared right now, and I won't be compassionate."

If I asked Neptune if he'd lied, I'd bet the answer would be negative. Which may or may not have been another lie. I was going to have to use the skills I'd learned to determine the truth because confrontational interrogation wasn't going to tell me what I wanted to know.

"Where are you going?" I asked.

"Other business."

"That's it? Pika is shaken up. You care about her. I know you do. Now would be a good time to show it."

"I want a full report."

I got mad. "Why do you need a report? You can hear everything I say over the comm device. Just go and do whatever it is you think is more important than showing Pika you care."

"The comm device is off, and it's going to stay off. Your friend hacked into it. It's been compromised. All further communication on this matter will be face to face."

"He can't hear you. Only I can hear you. And

Zeke at least has the courtesy to let me know when he's listening."

"All further communication will be face to face," he repeated.

"Fine. Where do you want to meet? I'm due for duty right here in about an hour, and Daila already told me she'll be conducting spontaneous check-ups. If I'm not here, she'll report me for not being at my post."

"Let me handle Daila."

"I don't want you to handle my boss. I can handle her myself."

He ignored that. "Get Pika a uniform. Rank of Ensign. I want her to look like an employee of this ship as much as she can. Your future on Moon Unit 6 depends on it."

I put my hands on my hips. "Why is it *you* broke the rules by sneaking your long-lost sister onto the ship to get her to Venus and *my* future is the one at stake?"

"Just do it." He turned around and stormed toward the HVPTS.

"You owe me, Neptune."

He turned his head slightly and said, "The same way you owed Zeke Champion?"

I did not humor him with a response.

When I returned to Pika, she was sitting up on the bench with her knees bent close to her chest. "Neptune's lonely," she said.

"I don't want to talk about Neptune. Tell me about Xina. You said she was your friend, right?"

Pika nodded. "She is my friend. She brings me presents and teaches me how to look like her, and —" she opened her eyes wide and clamped her hand over her mouth.

"What? It's okay, Pika. That's what girlfriends do. We can do those things too if you want. It's fun to play dress up." I went to the uniform closet and found the smallest orange shift dress in the inventory. "Let's start today. Put this on, and I'll alter it to fit you. You'll look like me."

"Okay."

I handed the uniform to Pika, and she dressed. As her fear dissipated, she slowly returned to her regular physical size.

Faced with the task of altering a uniform to fit her, I was afraid of taking in too much of the fabric, so I folded the excess on the sides and sealed it with High Durability Tape from my emergency alteration toolkit. The tape appeared white in normal light but had reflective pigments which would help in case of a blackout. Considering the various scares Pika had already had since being on the ship, I didn't mention that being a possibility.

I kept up small talk while fitting Pika's uniform, mostly to put her at ease and make sure her size was back to normal. Of all the talents in the universe, the Gremlons delighted in performing and getting a rise out of an audience, which made me wonder about Xina and whether Pika had ever performed for her.

"Tell me about your friendship with Xina," I said. "You two must have gotten to know each other pretty well after she visited Neptune. I never had the chance to meet her. What was she like?"

"She's sparkly and funny and pretty, but she has a secret that I'm not supposed to tell."

It pained me not to tell Pika that her friend was dead, but until Neptune indicated it was safe, I knew we couldn't mention Xina's death. Secrets fell within the territory of security team members—and the credentials Neptune had given me yesterday indicated that's what I now was. "Secrets are hard to keep, but it's okay. Neptune told me Xina's secret, so if you want to talk about it with me, you can. It'll be *our* secret."

"I don't think Neptune knows Xina's secret," she said.

"Yes, he does. He told me."

"But if Neptune knew Xina wasn't a real Venusian, then why'd he let her on the ship?"

"What do you mean, she's not a real Venusian?"

"She's not. She faked it with sparkles and sugar powder. Xina liked to play dress up just like me!"

15: WHEN A VENUSIAN IS NOT A VENUSIAN

VENUSIANS WERE EXOTIC BY NATURE, BUT IT wouldn't surprise me to learn that Xina had enhanced her looks with perfumes and powders from specialty shops. Just about anything imaginable could be bought somewhere in the galaxy if you knew where to look.

"She was probably just downplaying her appearance so you wouldn't feel different from her," I said. "And it was nice of her to share her powders with you." I remembered something. "Did you try to eat them? Is that why you burped up sparkles?"

"She said she used to be sparkly like the other Venusians, but sometimes she didn't feel well, and she had to use potions and powders to look like them. She ate them and poured them on her head and bathed in them! Xina liked all sorts of sparkly things. She has little sparkles and big sparkles and giant sparkles. I love playing with Xina's sparkles!"

The more Pika told me about Xina, the more I questioned whether Xina's "illness" was real, or if it was imposter syndrome. As in, Xina wasn't really a Venusian, and she'd faked her way into Neptune's trust. But that possibility scared me more than the original one because it meant the now deceased alien masquerading as Neptune's sister had had an agenda. And she'd used the head of Moon Unit 6 security to further it, and we'd broken a ton of security protocols to help keep it hidden.

It was a growing hunch that I couldn't shake. Neptune either already knew and was keeping the truth from me, or he didn't know, in which case I wasn't about to say anything until I had proof.

There was the additionally troubling fact that I was wearing the comm device and Neptune could hear everything I could hear. He'd said he turned it off, but what if he hadn't? Had he heard what Pika said? Did he believe it or dismiss it as the misperception of an innocent Gremlon who believed what she wanted to believe?

I went to the supply console and pulled out a big blue sugar pop, ran it under water to dissolve the sanitary casing, and handed it to Pika. She stuck it in her mouth eagerly. I took a cherry Anti-Vert pop out of the cabinet for myself to offset any residual wooziness from too many trips on the HVPTS.

Moments later, Pika finished her pop and smiled. Her teeth and lips were stained blue.

"Are you feeling better?" I asked.

"Yes, yes, yes!"

"Do you want to go to your quarters?"

"No, no, no."

"Why not?"

She blinked a couple of times and then jumped up from the bench and zipped to the other side of the room. Drat! I forgot how fast Gremlons were when they got cagey!

"Won't go, won't go, won't go!" she said.

"Why?"

She stuck out her bright blue bottom lip. "I'm scared of the meanie greenies."

"Pika, is your room near the communication deck?"

She nodded.

So that's how the Martians knew about Pika. A snapshot of her recent time on the ship was forming. She'd been bullied by a small group of Martians early on and had become terrified of all the little green men. Her fear made her vulnerable. Between my height and Hapkido skills, I wasn't afraid of them, but Pika was a different story. Gremlons lacked the instinct to defend themselves. It was why old Gremlons were rarely seen—

because they had zero self-preservation instincts and, when faced with a threat, chose playing dead over fighting for their lives. Too often, they became the victims of mass annihilation or casualties of space war.

If Pika's room was near the Martians, she'd avoid them at all costs. And if that meant hiding in someone else's quarters, she'd do it. I was but one of her friends on this ship. Xina was the other. The presence of sparkles in and on Pika told me exactly where she'd been hiding out.

Neptune hadn't said where he was going, but I'd bet it was Xina's room. Pika had been in there. Someone else could have been in there too. Someone who suspected Xina didn't belong and wanted to discover her secret. I didn't know why she'd been eliminated yet, and that limited what I could determine about her killer. Was the murderer a jealous passenger who wanted the grand prize? Or someone who knew about her relationship to Neptune? Did it have to do with her illness? Or was there something else?

At the space academy, enemy motive and assessment had been a third-year course. I'd tested out of the pre-courses, and the professor had signed off on my petition to take it early. There we'd learned a formula for solving this kind of problem. It involved identifying variables and plotting them like a star chart. The first variable was when the crime was committed. Next was who was present at that time. Third was to list what we knew about the victim. The points, once mapped out, would intersect: the killer. It was T+S+V=K. Time plus suspects plus victim equals killer.

Anatol's report was due soon. Once that report reached Captain Ryder, more people would be asking questions, and Neptune and my time would be spent on containment.

If Neptune went to Xina's quarters, he would have found the same evidence that Pika was telling me about: the topical creams, powders, gels, and other sparkles that she used to appear Venusian. The wardrobe that would have perpetuated the confusion, and maybe even something more concrete. It was entirely possible Neptune already knew what Pika had told me. But one thing was for sure: despite Xina's quarters being a perfectly acceptable hideout for Pika while Xina was alive, based on what had happened, it was now 100 percent off limits.

"You're going to stay with me for the rest of the trip. You can play with Cat if you want, okay? He's all better, and he misses you."

"He does?"

"Of course, he does. Why wouldn't he?"

"Because I broke him."

"Cat is very forgiving when it comes to things like that."

Cat was a robotic pet that I built from spare parts on Plunia. I'd pieced together discarded circuits from radio receivers, transmitters, and recording devices, programmed a hundred and seventy-five executable commands, and a handful of feline-centric behaviors for kicks. He'd been a little worse for wear after Pika discovered him on the last moon trek, but like any good tomcat, he recovered with a little TLC (and some circuit modifications) and was back in action (in the confines of my closet). I balled up the Venusian cape and buried it in the bottom of the uniform ward laundry cart.

Pika and I got all the way to my quarters before static filled my ear. Apparently, my vacation from Neptune was over. "I thought you turned this thing off?" I said.

"Sylvia, it's Zeke."

"You have to stop contacting me on my comm device! Neptune thinks—never mind what Neptune thinks. This isn't a good idea."

"This has to do with Neptune. Sylvia, you have to find a way to get me onto your ship."

"You're joking, right? We're on our way to Venus. I don't even know if this ship is equipped with a working rematerliaizer."

"Listen to me. You know the files I swapped from Moon Unit Medi-Bay?"

"Yes."

"When I covered up the ones that were there, I kept a copy of the originals for myself. The Venusian on your ship wasn't a Venusian. She was an imposter."

"I know. I didn't know when I talked to you earlier, but I know now."

"You've got bigger problems than that. Your murdered imposter was an escaped convict from Colony 13. Her official arrest record says she was convicted for murdering a federation guard during the commission of a crime. There's no way Neptune's going to get away with pulling strings to get her on board. He aided and abetted a criminal."

16: CODE WORD: TOGETHERNESS

"Xina killed a federation guard?" I asked. "What else do you know?"

"The details are classified, but I cross-referenced the known factors about her to the major crimes committed during her lifetime and came up with a biggie. The black carbonado diamonds were stolen from the Intergalactic Supernova Museum right around the time she was arrested. A federation guard was killed. Sylvia, I'm pretty sure Xina was the one who pulled the trigger."

"What happened to the diamonds?"

"Nobody knows."

Neptune had said something about chipping. A science experiment on cross-breeding. A controlled environment. All babies from the trial were tagged with tracking chips embedded at the base of their skulls. If Xina was chipped as a baby, then how had she participated in the commission of a robbery? I knew from Pika that Xina had enhanced her natural appearance to play up the Venusian angle. But Xina being an escaped convict from Colony 13? That was a surprise.

A surprise that would be included in Commander Anatol's report to the captain if the science officer had done his job—but I had no idea what information he had accessed: the DNA of the victim or the junk DNA Zeke had uploaded at my request.

"Hold on a second," I said. I pulled Cat out of the closet and handed him to Pika. "Play nice." She wrapped both of her arms around the white robot kitty in an affectionate hug.

I turned my back on Pika and spoke to Zeke. "Are you there?"

"Yes. What's wrong?"

"The second in command of the ship was tasked to investigate Xina's murder. Is there any way to find out if he accessed her medical files yet and if so, which ones he got?"

"He requisitioned them from Medi-Morgue, but Doc told him he has to wait. There was a rash of illness linked to some tainted protein packs in the crew vending machines and Medi-Bay's currently filled to capacity."

"Why didn't I hear anything about that?" I asked.

"Have you eaten in the crew mess hall?"

"No. I was at First Dinner, and I haven't eaten since."

"It seems someone interrupted the power source on the vending machines and the protein turned. Anybody who ate in there in the past couple of hours is in or on their way to Medi-Bay."

I could name one crew who could have been responsible but satisfying my curiosity could wait for later. "How much time do I have before Anatol gets those test results?"

"Well, now that the tainted food source was identified, anybody who didn't eat the protein won't, so Medi-Bay won't continue to fill up. That means when Doc finishes treating the crew he has now, he'll be all caught up. Whoever unplugged the vending machines and let the protein packs go bad bought you a couple of hours minimum. Maybe a day."

"And then what?"

"And then Doc moves on to Xina's medical panels and gives Anatol what he wants."

"A couple of hours to a day, then," I stated.

"Yep."

"Thanks, Zeke. Stryker out."

I sat down and pieced Zeke's new information with what I already knew. Colony 13 was part of M-13, a stretch of thirteen colonies under Federation Council rule. When the galaxy was sliced up into territories, the council established Colony 13 to quarantine convicts, outcasts, and prisoners. Tracking chips monitored the whereabouts and compliance of residents, who traded their personal data for the illusion of freedom. Occasionally a chip surfaced on the black market, one that had been surgically removed. Removal of a tracking chip was punishable in an unfortunate way: nine times out of ten, the surgery led to death. There were those to whom the risk was worth it.

Considering the severity of my dad's crimes, he would have been a prime candidate for chipping. At the time, he'd been sentenced to restricted confinement in the Federation Council penitentiary. I didn't know what had become of him after the FC took him away. For all I knew, they kept him locked up to save themselves the cost of the chip.

The comm device buzzed in my ear. "Sylvia? Me again." Considering he wasn't officially part of Moon Unit 6 staff, I overlooked Zeke's informal communication style. "We forgot to talk about getting me onto your ship."

"I just told you that's not possible."

"Listen carefully. I accessed Moon Unit 6's flight plan. It's scheduled to go on autopilot through an upcoming asteroid minefield. I'll take my dad's repair pod and run a parallel flight plan with a 7 percent intercept angle. All you have to do is open the hatch at the designated time."

"Are you kidding me? I can't open the hatch on a moving ship."

"Yes, you can. Tell your captain you detected a problem. Get her to issue a work order. I'll dispatch repair drones to back up your story. They can run an exterior check as a diversion."

Zeke's idea was crazy, but it could work. The ship would have to cancel engines while the drones completed an in-flight diagnostic report, and the perfect time to cancel forward thrust was while we were floating through an asteroid minefield.

"Walk me through your plan," I said.

"You open the hatch, let me on, and seal the hatch."

"Can't you do it by remote access like you did with the computer?"

"No. The system will detect the violation and issue an alert to the corporate offices. It has to be done from a ship computer and even then, we have to take precautions. I'll override the immediate history in the flight memory. The drones will complete the exterior diagnostics, the ship will get a clean check, and Moon Unit 6 can resume its trek to Venus."

"There's one problem," I said. "Only two members on this ship have the override codes to the hatch. Neptune and Anatol."

"Not the captain?"

"If something happens to the ship, the captain is expected to stay with it. The second in command is in charge of the safety of the passengers. That's Anatol."

"How well do you know him?"

I thought about Anatol's investigation. "Getting Anatol to cooperate is going to be a problem."

"That leaves one choice." Zeke was quiet for a moment. "Neptune."

"I knew who you meant."

"Is he going to play ball?"

"I have no idea."

And then a third voice came over the comm device. "Stryker. My quarters. Now."

It *figured* Neptune lied about cutting off communication to my comm device!

"Zeke Champion out."

The comm device went silent.

17: NEPTUNE'S QUARTERS

I ACTIVATED CAT'S MIRROR MODE AND SLIPPED out of the room while Pika swatted at Cat's raised paw. I got into the corner HVPTS and hesitated for a moment. I didn't know where Neptune's quarters were. I punched in the code for security section. The pressure burst under my feet and seconds later I tumbled onto the concrete and into Neptune's legs.

"This is security section," he said. "I said my quarters."

"Then what are you doing here?"

"I told you to meet me—never mind. Come on."

"Where are we going?"

He put his muscular arm around my waist and picked me up. Even with gravity boots on he lifted me easily. In four strides we were back at the HVPTS.

"I'm not going back in there already. My equilibrium is off, and we won't both fit, and I need another Anti-Vert Pop—"

Neptune set me down. He wrapped both arms around me and held me tight against his broad chest. I turned my head to breathe. His hold restricted my ability to fight against him or wriggle free—not that there would have been room for a fight if I wanted to. Together we barely fit. "Sector 7," he said. The seal slipped into place, the pressure exploded under our feet, and the transport system launched us.

Every single time I'd taken that darn high velocity pressure transport system, I'd been spit out of the tube in a pile on the ground. Neptune's arms held me upright. But there were other side effects of being this close to Neptune. A hum vibrated throughout my body, and with my ear pressed against his chest, I was hyper-aware of his strong heartbeat. The other times I'd taken the HVPTS, the temperature in the tube had been cool. This time, heat scaled the back of my neck, and my skin got bright.

The HPVTS released us. Neptune landed on his feet and kept his arms around me.

"Tell me when you're stable," he said, his lips grazing my ear.

"I'm stable."

"I'm not going to let go until I'm sure."

I was acutely aware of Neptune's closeness. His scent reminded me of moon dust and fresh figs. I leaned against his chest and counted to three.

He let go at two and a half. "You're milking it."

The action snapped me out of otherwise distracting thoughts. "Me? You're the one who wouldn't let go." I brushed imaginary Neptune cooties from the surface of my uniform.

"Stryker," he said.

"I'm fine. I've been standing on my own since I was a little purple toddler."

"Stryker," he said again.

"What?" The tone of his voice was different from the usual gruff way he said my name. I shifted my attention from my uniform to his face.

"I'm in trouble and I need your help."

"If you've been listening in on my private conversations then you know I already know that. You could have trusted me," I said. "With the truth. You could have told me the truth from the beginning."

"No, I couldn't."

"Why not?"

"Because I didn't know the truth until tonight."

"How is that possible? You're you. You don't trust anything you hear until you confirm it from four different sources."

"Xina's story was different. I believed her."

Because he'd wanted to. Neptune, the toughest

124

man in the universe, had wanted to believe that he could save his sister. It broke my half human heart. For all of Neptune's back channels, passwords, and secret missions, he'd had the wool pooled over his eyes by a sick Venusian posing as his long-lost, genetically-enhanced sibling. I guess it could have happened to anybody.

"Tell me about Xina showing up on your doorstep," I said.

"We don't have time."

"Well then we better *make* time. First rule of any mission is to establish the emotional risks and weaknesses of members of the team and calibrate the mission accordingly. You were tricked by a fake Venusian. The Neptune I know wouldn't have been. I want to know why."

"Sit down."

For the first time since we'd been dumped from the HVPTS, I looked at our surroundings. The room was gray. Dark, matte gray. A cot lay along one wall. It was gray. The floor was coated in the same magnetic paint that had been used in the holding cell in security section. The walls, the cabinet, and the items strewn about were all gray.

"What is this place?"

"My quarters."

"No wonder you spend so much time in security section. I wouldn't want to spend any time here either." I looked for a place to sit down, but the only option was the cot. I stared at it for a couple of seconds, the thermal blanket taut across the surface like they trained cadets to do in the military academy. Pillows were propped along the far wall. I wasn't sure if I was comfortable sitting on Neptune's bed, even if he had told me he didn't sleep.

"Sit down," he said again.

I sat on the corner of his cot. His eyes darkened, and his lips parted ever so slightly. Heat climbed the back of my neck again. I stood up. "You could have requested a chair or two from the design crew. For entertaining guests. You *are* a senior officer of the ship."

Neptune picked me up and set me on top of his table. He sat on the cot in front of me. His head was eye-level with my knees, which had spread slightly when he planted me in this position. I pressed my knees together, and he stood up from the cot and turned his back on me.

"I don't entertain," he said over his shoulder.

"You're entertaining me."

"Are you entertained right now?"

"Not exactly."

"My point."

I jumped up and grabbed his arm, trying to turn him around. "Neptune, it doesn't matter if I'm sitting or standing, if we're facing each other or in two different rooms. You have a problem. You came to me, remember? I don't know why, but I'm here, which I think means I'm on the very short list of people you think can help you. Stop wasting time being stubborn and trust me."

He turned. "You don't know why I came to you?"

"No, I don't. Maybe you finally succumbed to my considerable Plunian charms."

He took two steps forward and placed his hands on my shoulders, squaring me off so I couldn't look anywhere but directly at him. Despite the futility of the gesture, I put my hands on his thick forearms to push them off. They didn't budge. My purple skin, which had cooled to a soft lavender in my room, now glowed like I'd been injected with radium.

As much as I'd tried to deny it, the electrical current between Neptune and me was unmistakable—and on my part, visible. Neptune didn't pay attention to anybody else on the ship the way he paid attention to me. I would never have spoken to another senior officer the way I spoke to him, and he never said a word about it. He treated me like, well, like I was a pain in his butt, but one that he tolerated for reasons unspoken. And here we were, alone in his quarters, and a new kind of energy had been introduced into the room.

Being part Earthling meant I had my share of unpredictable emotions, ones I fought to keep under wraps around strangers. Through a series of mental exercises, I strengthened my powers of recall until I was top of my class. I could rebuild a Plunian potato fryer or a Moon Unit thrust enabler in less time than it took Pika to bounce from one side of the uniform ward to the other. I could identify if someone was lying in under five seconds by recognizing the fifty-seven verity tells that I'd been trained on before I dropped out of school. But when I was excited, I couldn't stop myself from glowing in the dark.

"Can you control that?" Neptune asked.

"No."

He kept his hands in place a moment longer and then let go. My hands fell off his forearms. My skin slowly turned back to its natural shade. I was off-the-charts embarrassed. I was in Neptune's chambers because of a mission, not my sex drive.

"It's Venus," he said. "The closer we get to the planet, the more often that's going to happen."

"No, it's me. Something to do with the genetic mixture of Earthling and Plunian genes. Sometimes I get—turbocharged."

"Have you ever been to Venus?"

"No."

"I went. During the break between Moon Units. I told you I went looking for my sister, and that's where I went looking. The whole planet is —turbocharged."

What was he trying to tell me? While I spent my break bunking with Zeke in a vacant dormitory outside Space Academy, he'd gotten his freak on with a bunch of oversexed aliens?

"Forget my condition," I said. "It's an inconvenient side effect of being half Plunian. I'm mostly back to normal."

"I'm not."

"You're as normal as you were five minutes ago—not that you're normal, but you didn't light up like a glowstick, so consider yourself lucky."

"I have other physical changes around you. That's why I went to Venus."

I put my hands up in front of me. "TMI, Neptune. What you do in your private time is your business."

"Stryker," he said. "I watched you lose everything. I saw what that did to you. For the first time in my life, I saw a person on the edge, prepared to sacrifice everything she had left and succumb to the darkness inside of her because she thought it could save someone else."

"It would have saved a lot of someone elses," I said quietly. "You know what they teach us at the academy. The needs of the many—"

"It would have saved me. Until that moment, I didn't think I deserved to be saved." My skin started to glow again. Neptune stepped back and put more space between us. "Venus is an adult vacation destination for a reason. Between the climate, air quality, and subsonic rhythms that were released when the third moon formed, there's a unique atmosphere."

"Unique?"

"Heady. Intoxicating. Almost hallucinogenic. Federation Council established zoning regulations to make the planet safe for visitors, but you can't help but feel the effects the closer you get."

"What kind of effects?"

"Let's just say you're more inclined to drop your inhibitions."

Until now, I didn't know Neptune *had* inhibitions. But the issue he described was more significant than that. A planet that encouraged people to act without thinking would be dangerous. Security work required control. We'd been tested on it to varying degrees at the academy. Ten levels. Anyone who didn't get past five was immediately reassigned to a different specialty.

"You've never struck me as the type who wants to be out of control. Tell me again why you went?"

"It was necessary to pick up the trail of my sister. I watched you lose everything when Plunia exploded. Before that moment, you had family. Space pirates took them away, not you. I had family out there somewhere, and I'd turned my back on her. You didn't have a choice about being alone. I did."

"But according to Zeke, Xina wasn't your sister. According to Pika, Xina showed up looking for you, not the other way around. And I have reason to believe Xina wasn't even Venusian. Maybe she was a little, but she enhanced her appearance with powders and potions and sparkles. Did she put a whammy on you? Is that how she got you to arrange for her to be on this ship?"

"You're only partly right. Xina was a convict from Colony 13. She was one of the babies born in the experiment. I found her after receiving some intel and arranged for her to be on this ship for one reason. She may have not been my sister, but she knew where my sister was. Every string I pulled to get Xina Astryd onto this ship was a means to an end."

18: GANG GREEN

"I need more facts, Neptune," I said. "Every time you change the story on me, I start to wonder what else you're hiding."

He turned away. "My real sister's name is Vesta. Space pirates took her from us when I was in school. I found a source who confirmed that she's alive."

"What does Xina have to do with your sister?"

"Xina was slowly dying from the malfunctioning chip in her head. There's a doctor on Venus who can remove the chip for a price."

"What price?"

"Not my concern."

I stood up. "We have too many problems to operate under crisis management. We have to treat this as a mission. You heard Zeke on my comm. He has a plan. We need to bring him into the team and hear him out."

"No."

"Yes. Your number one priority is the safety of Vesta, right? Your real sister? That means every decision you make will be with that endgame in mind. I can't make those decisions. If we have to go to Venus to get her—and if Venus affects people the way you say it does—then you can't do this alone. You need me. And for you to complete your mission, you are going to need interference. That's where Zeke comes in. He's smart. He's talented," I ticked Zeke's strengths off on my fingers. "And he already knows more than you want him to know and I won't let you kill him to keep your secrets quiet."

He grabbed my wrist and twisted my arm backward. "How do you plan to stop me?"

Instinctively, I relaxed into the direction Neptune twisted my arm instead of fighting back. I channeled my energy into a ball inside me, coiled, and then released with a sweeping kick that caught him off guard. His legs shot out from under him. He toppled. He kept his grip tight on my arm and yanked me toward him. I tucked my head and flipped in a somersault over top of him. His arm extended until his shoulder snapped. He released me. I landed on the floor past him with the soles of my boots against the wall. I pushed off into a backward flip and stood, unsure if my demonstration of Hapkido skills had made things better or worse.

From the looks of Neptune's shoulder, I'd made things worse. It was dislocated. His arm dangled by his side. He stood and moved to the cabinet on the far wall and twisted his torso, slamming into the sturdy frame. When he turned to face me, his shoulder was back in joint.

"You didn't yell," I said. "You just slammed your dislocated shoulder into a cabinet, and you didn't make a sound."

"Where'd you learn to fight?"

"Around."

He raised one eyebrow. Then he pulled a dry ice pack out of the gray freezer, smacked it on the surface of the desk, and held it against his shoulder. "Call Zeke Champion."

"I don't have to call him," I said. "I'm pretty sure he's been listening this whole time." I turned away from Neptune. "Zeke?" There was no answer. I tapped my ear. "Zeke?" I looked at Neptune. "Great. It's broken."

"It's not broken. I jammed his frequency." Neptune pulled his computer tablet from the docking station and typed in a series of characters. "Go."

"Zeke? Are you there?"

"Geez, Sylvia! What happened?"

"We don't have time for small talk. Neptune's

on board with your plan. What do you need?"

"Moon Unit 6 will be at the asteroid minefield by Zulu Four tomorrow. Your first step will be to talk to your captain and get her to initiate a work order for repair drones. I'll intercept the order from my dad's computer and take it from there."

"That gives us a little over a day. Is that enough time?"

"It's going to have to be. You have one window, and that's it."

I watched Neptune. He pursed his lips and nodded. "Zulu Four is good. The crew and passengers will be asleep. We'll have the hatch resealed before anybody can detect the infraction."

"What about Pika?" I asked. "She's asleep in my quarters, but you know how Gremlons are. She could get into a lot of trouble by then."

"Leave Pika to me," Neptune said. "What's your risk assessment?"

"Aside from my responsibilities in the uniform ward, everything else is unpredictable. Martians, medical teams, criminal records, chipped passengers, fake Venusians, real Venusians, little kids running around the spaceship, and a possible public relations scandal that could bring down Moon Unit Corporation—"

"Not to mention the way you glow when you say Neptune's name," Zeke said.

"Zeke, Neptune can hear you."

"Whoops."

But yeah, add that to the mix. Looked like I'd be wearing Stealthyester® for the duration of the trip.

There was no point hanging around Neptune's quarters. I was tired and hungry, and while proximity to him provided an unusual distraction, it wasn't going to help in the long run. Besides, my mission was clear. Invent a plausible problem with the ship that required repair drones and inform Captain Ryder. There was a full day until we reached the asteroid minefield, and too much could happen in that time to make our whole plan fall apart.

I happily took the passenger walkway to my room. Neptune's quarters hadn't been listed on the schematics, and I took a few wrong turns before I recognized where I was. Unfortunately, that recognition came with the presence of several small green Martians. Bottol led the group.

"Would you look at what we have here," he said.

"Back off, Martian. I'm not in the mood."

"Maybe we can help you with that." There was snickering amongst the group. "Shouldn't you be off babysitting the Gremlon?" he continued.

"She's all grown up. She can take care of herself."

"Sure," he said. "And while she's taking care of herself, you can take care of all of us."

"Green isn't my color." Confident that I could take them down as easily as I had the day we departed, I walked right up to the group. "Now let me through, boys."

The pack of green men parted. As I passed through, the scent of Jupiter Juice, an acrid strain of cheap alcohol that was easy to distill and even easier to obtain wafted through the air. The Martians were drunk. Their smaller stature caused alcohol to metabolize rapidly, and a pleasant drunk could turn surly fast. Bottol's lewd suggestion made more sense in the context of his intoxication, but if the Martian's mood turned toward retribution for the fight in the hallway, there were enough of them to easily overpower me.

As I walked down the hall, I listened for sounds behind me. There were no reflective surfaces to indicate whether I was being followed or not and turning to check would indicate my fear and vulnerability. When I'd shown up to help Pika, I'd taken the HVPTS, but the HVPTS was not regulation, and hopping into it without cause or command would give the Martians reason to report me. I had to fly under the radar until Zeke was safely on board. That was the mission. The mission was greater than me.

The first strike hit my knees. They buckled, and I fell forward onto the carpet. Small green hands grabbed at my ankles and dragged me backward into a white room. The doors closed. I kicked my feet to free myself. One of the Martians straddled my neck and pushed my face into the carpet. I gasped for breath and inhaled carpet fibers. Immediately, I coughed. My head was pulled up and an inhaler was jammed into my mouth. A stream of contaminated air filled me. I gasped for breath while my lungs convulsed. Laughter surrounded me. Tiny green hands pulled my arms and legs out in each direction. I was conscious, but my muscles wouldn't react to my need to fight. I couldn't cry for help with the inhaler held in place. The hands moved up the back of my thighs, and my stomach clenched at the horror of what the angry Martians were about to do.

19: AN UNLIKELY ALLY

THE DOORS SWISHED OPEN. THE SCENT OF SPUN sugar replaced the smell of alcohol. "This is highly unusual," said a male voice.

"Go away," snarled Bottol. "We saw her first."

The Martian who held the inhaler in my mouth was distracted. I spit out the inhaler. "Help me," I said in a barely audible whisper.

"She does not want you. Leave."

The grabbing and biting ceased. The Martian on my neck climbed off me as well. I turned my head and watched the little green men retreat from the room to the hallway where we'd been. Towering above them—above me—was Synn, the Venusian male who'd performed in the Space Bar during First Dinner. Surrounding his head was a halo of sparkle dust which only added to his aura of savior.

"You are the uniform lieutenant," he said. "You dined with the captain."

I rolled onto my back and inhaled clean, oxygenated, non-carpet fiber air. Exhaled. Repeated. Twice. "Yes," I said.

The tall Venusian held his hand down to me. "I am Synn."

"I'm Sylvia." I took his hand and pulled myself up to a sitting position. "Thank you."

"On my planet, that was a crime."

"On my planet too," I said. (If I still had a planet.)

"Then why do you thank me?"

"Because the Martians were—I didn't want them to—what do you think was the crime?"

"Interrupting you with your suitors."

I choked on my response. "Those Martians were no suitors. They knocked me down and dragged me out of the hallway. I don't know what would have happened if you hadn't arrived." The color returned to my skin and, as my terror subsided, I stood. "How did you know we were in here?"

"I watched you from a viewing station on the observation deck," he said. "Your behavior was curious."

As was his. I wasn't going to question his motives, because his presence had kept a scary situation from becoming a nightmare of a memory, but there was something creepy about his willingness to watch the Martians attack me.

"Well, thank you again," I said. "You're right, what you saw was curious. It's also cause for expulsion from the ship if reported, so you may be called upon by the senior crew to tell what you saw here."

"I don't understand," he said. "The Martians will report me for interrupting?"

"Not the Martians. Me."

"You will report me for interrupting the Martians?"

"No. I will report the Martians for what they were about to do to me."

Synn's face indicated serenity. "But there is nothing unusual about the Martian behavior. It happens on Venus all the time. We are a loving people." He ran his fingertip up his arm, and small sparkles fluttered off and spun around in the light. "We encourage love. We don't report it."

"What you walked in on wasn't love," I said.

Synn seemed lost in his thoughts. He closed his eyes. A few seconds later, the door opened and Shyrr entered. I left before they got any ideas of their own.

The conversation with Synn left my thoughts muddled. That wasn't my first run-in with Martians, but it was the most unnerving. Yet the Venusian thought it was perfectly normal.

The Martians were employees like I was. That

meant they'd passed background checks and been approved by Moon Unit Corp. Plunians and Martians tended not to get along, and now that I was removed from the immediate threat of them, I honestly didn't know if the trigger had merely been a desire for revenge fueled by Jupiter Juice. I had experience being ostracized thanks to my dad. I needed to think about this a little more before I acted.

Despite the sudden attraction of all the HVPTS had to offer in terms of anonymous and rapid travel throughout the ship, I kept to the passenger corridors and reached my quarters within the hour. Pika was asleep in my bed. Cat was on the pillow next to her, and they were nose to nose. Traces of the topical sparkle cream had rubbed off Pika and transferred onto my pillowcase. I left both Cat and Pika sleeping in the dark (the light would trigger Cat's wake up meow), stripped out of my uniform, and stepped into the deionization chamber to rinse off the memory of the little green hands.

Until tonight, I'd felt secure in my ability to defend myself. I'd taken down Neptune with a sweeping kick. And the Martians, while numerous, were two feet shorter than I was. It hadn't occurred to me that they had come up with their own ways of fighting. I didn't know what was in the inhaler they'd forced into my mouth, but anything less than

79 percent oxygen would have left me incapacitated. Any false sense of confidence I'd had was gone.

It also troubled me to remember that they'd been trying to access Xina's records when Zeke was on our network. Why? Did they have something to do with her murder? I already knew she'd struck a deal with Neptune to get her to a doctor who could remove her tracking chip, but had she put all her trust in Neptune, or was she playing him along with the Martians and anybody else who would listen? Was this about his sister, or was it a trap to get him?

I swallowed two oxygen tablets and secured my small, emergency canister of O2 to my thigh under my Stealthyester® gear. From my locker, I pulled out a silver package of Plunian potatoes. After not having eaten for several hours, protein would have been the smart choice, but I needed comfort food. Zeke's dad kept a supply of vacuum-packed foods on hand for use when he was called on intergalactic ship repair jobs, and Zeke had let me raid the storage closet the night he found me crying over my mom's death.

That was the only time I'd let myself cry. The rage, the loss, the act of pretending to be strong, had been too much to bear. I hadn't wanted a friend to know I succumbed to human emotions, and I left the privacy of the bunk wrapped in a blanket and sat outside staring at the sky. It was my way of consoling myself. I was as isolated as anybody, but the vastness of space told me I'd never be completely alone. Out there in the universe were countless other sob stories like mine.

As I munched on the potatoes, I thought about Neptune's sister Vesta. He was so intent to find her that he could be walking into a trap. Someone could be using his desire to find her get him to break the law. Neptune had been pushed to cross the boundaries that had been instilled in him. And he said it was because of me.

I didn't know how I felt about that.

Except, in a very small way, I did. Because for the first time since learning I'd lost everything I'd ever known, I saw that my loss had affected someone else.

Training at the space academy had been about becoming a soldier. My focus had been security, because I had an analytical mind and the skills to rebuild, repair, and remember things. My rate of retention still held the record even though I'd never graduated. More than one student since me had lobbied to have my name abolished from the record board for that reason, but despite what the faculty felt about my dropping out, they never undermined my accomplishments.

Being trained in security measures meant being willing to sacrifice anything for a mission and being able to work as a team. My family was gone. Thanks to my dad's crime, most of my friends had abandoned me too. But on Moon Unit 6, I was part of something bigger than me. Yes, it was a cruise ship, not nearly as respected as a ship that engaged in space exploration or enforced military law, but it had a crew, and I was part of it. Yet none of that mattered, because when the mission to save Vesta required me to break a few rules, I didn't think twice. The team was my lifeline, and Neptune was on my team.

Zeke too, as long as his plan to board the ship worked. If it didn't, his blood would be on my hands.

I knew how I felt about that, and I'd do everything in my power to ensure success. I wasn't losing one of the few friends I had.

I left my quarters and went to the uniform ward for two reasons: access to my computer and a place to sleep. The corridors of the ship were quiet. I wore my bubble helmet, more for the safety net of guaranteed oxygen than because it was convenient.

Over an hour had passed since meeting with Neptune. This time tomorrow, if everything went as planned, Zeke would be on board the ship. If Zeke were successful, Anatol wouldn't find anything of note on his report of Xina's death. If we pulled off our plan, Moon Unit 6 would continue our trek to Venus.

That was a whole lot of ifs.

Once in the uniform ward, I activated a mission detail log and filled in the blanks.

Task 1: Notify captain of threat.

Task 2:

Wait. I couldn't notify Captain Ryder of a threat until I made up a threat. I overrode the first task with *Identify threat* and moved *Notify captain* to Task 2. From that point, everything was up in the air. If she issued the work order as we expected, we could continue. If she didn't, we'd need a new plan. Everything rode on my initial report.

Good thing I work well under pressure.

I split my computer screen, pulling up the plans of the ship on the left and mapping our flight plan on the right. We were currently traveling at a speed of 25,000 miles per hour, but our flight plan indicated a slower velocity before passengers started rising and occupying the observation deck. I scanned ahead and found what Zeke had seen. The mapped asteroid mine, the variables that projected when we'd enter it, and the commands that had already been programmed into the thrusters to slow us to a non-lethal speed to navigate through the minefield. So far, so good.

I maximized the window with the schematics and rotated the illustrations three hundred and sixty degrees to find the best possible place to report damage. Moon Unit 6 was fresh from the factory floor and had been made using the newest materials and the latest technology. *Anything* I reported was going to seem unusual and suspicious.

Whatever I reported to the captain would need to be backed up by two additional channels: photographic images from the cameras mounted on the exterior of the ship, and an error report triggered from a scheduled security sweep. I could hack the computer and write an error report, but without photographic evidence, it would appear suspicious. And photographic evidence without an error report wouldn't make sense either. I needed both and I needed them within minutes of each other.

Which meant I needed help.

And I knew the perfect person to ask.

20: RISKY BUSINESS

I RADIOED THE BRIDGE. "UNIFORM WARD TO bridge. Lieutenant Stryker requesting a meeting with Commander Anatol."

"Anatol here. What is the nature of the problem?"

"Confidential, sir. Request meeting face to face."

"Meet me in Council Chambers immediately. Over and out."

I used the HVPTS and arrived before Anatol. What I was about to do was either inspired or would bring our entire secret operation crashing down around our feet. If Neptune were listening in and thought this was a horrible idea, he would have said so. Which meant, for now, I was either on my own, or he was following along to see how my plan played out.

Council Chambers could only be opened by a senior officer, so I stood outside the room waiting for Anatol to arrive. He rounded the corner shortly thereafter.

"Lieutenant Stryker," he said.

"Commander Anatol," I returned.

He pressed his palm print on the scanner outside the room, and the doors slid open. Once we were inside with the doors closed behind me, Anatol faced me directly. "Your report, Lieutenant."

Thanks to my experience with Neptune's all work, no play communication style, I wasn't surprised by Anatol's directness.

"Earlier this evening, I saw what appeared to be a fire outside the rocket nozzle. I was on OB Two. I returned to the uniform ward and accessed the flight history and saw that we passed several comets. I believe one of the comets may have set fire to the exterior of the ship."

"An exterior fire cannot sustain itself in space," Anatol said. "The fire will have already extinguished."

"Except the rocket nozzle is directly above the beryllium spheres we keep on board the ship for emergency fuel," I said. "The fire could have transferred heat to the spheres through the aluminum exterior. Beryllium has a high heat capacity, so even if it picked up only a fraction of the heat from the comet fire, it would feed on itself and cause interior damage."

Anatol shifted his position from hands folded in front of him to arms crossed over his chest. His lack of immediate reply indicated he was considering my intel and not dismissing it outright. He was smart enough to know what I said was possible, and if it were possible, then it would need to be checked.

Even better, if Anatol issued the work order, he'd be preoccupied with the oversight of the repair drones and wouldn't be able to finish his report on Xina. Scientific knowledge for the win!

"What is your suggested course of action?" Anatol asked.

"The flight plan indicates we're headed for an asteroid mine. The ship could turn off engines, which would minimize the heat index, and a fleet of repair drones could do the work before we reach the other side."

Anatol turned away from me and picked up one of the tablet computers from the charging station. He inserted the tablet into the portal on the table and placed his hand on the screen. His credentials pulsed across it and a keyboard appeared on the lower portion of the display. He pulled up the schematics and tapped the rocket nozzle. It magnified and glowed orange just like it would have if it were overheated. Just like I'd said. Just like I'd programmed into the computer before leaving the uniform ward, just in case he did exactly this.

Anatol relaxed his crossed arms and nodded. "I'll issue the work order at once,"

he said. "That will be all, Lieutenant."

I nodded and exited Council Chambers. That was the second time I'd been there since the ship had departed and so far, so good. Plus, I hadn't had to rely on a favor from the captain—a favor that would have raised eyebrows (on those who had them) amongst crew members who already thought she gave me special treatment because of our shared biology.

I headed back toward the uniform ward reveling in my success. Anatol hadn't even cued up the exterior cameras to confirm my report or called to Ofra Starr in engineering to see if his staff could investigate the problem. But before I could question that too closely, I heard my name.

I turned around and saw Anatol standing in the middle of the corridor. "Good work." He paused for a moment. "You are overqualified for the uniform assignment."

"Thank you, Commander."

"I'll speak to the captain about having you retasked to a more suitable position on board Moon Unit 6."

"That won't be necessary. I'm very happy with the position I hold."

"The uniform lieutenant won't be able to join me in the rocket nozzle to oversee the drones. I imagine that would be of interest to someone with your background."

And it would. Under any other circumstances, I would have given my spare O_2 canister to observe the drones at work. But this was a problem. Anatol planned to keep an eye on me while the repairs were happening, which meant I couldn't be at the escape hatch to let Zeke onto the ship. Worse, when Anatol saw the beryllium spheres up close, he would know nothing I said was true.

And he'd wonder why I lied.

And Zeke wouldn't be able to override Xina's panel.

And Anatol would resume his investigation and discover Xina was an imposter.

And Neptune would be arrested for fixing the contest results and breaking a handful of rules.

And he'd never find his sister.

It was this last point that affected me the most. Neptune had only gone to look for Vesta after watching me lose everything. Not once in my entire life had my experiences motivated someone to take a path they might otherwise not have chosen. Especially someone like Neptune. Success for him would make my tragedy have meaning. In a roundabout way, Neptune's success in finding his sister would be a success for me too.

"In the meantime," Anatol continued, "return to your assignment. I'll be in touch."

I thanked the commander and headed back to the uniform ward. By all accounts, Neptune had heard our conversation. I waited to hear his voice, but it never came.

The peaceful quiet of the uniform ward allowed me to catch a couple hours of sleep. When I woke, my brain began the cycle it had only temporarily put on pause. It worked better than Cat's programmed alarm.

Until someone else was appointed to the uniform ward, I felt responsible for the duties, and the accumulated work would provide a necessary distraction. The laundry bin contained a few soiled uniforms on top of the sparkly cape I'd hidden in there. I stretched the crew garments onto screens and slid the screens into sanitation machines. One shirt was torn, which would require a replacement. I removed a fresh uniform from the inventory, logged it into the computer under the crew member's ID, and sealed it in a transport tube. The tubes worked much like the HVPTS except on a significantly smaller scale—tubes could only accommodate what would fit in the small three-inch diameter cylinders that were designed for such purpose. I fitted the cylinder into the tube, keyed the crew member's ID into the keypad, and activated the chamber. The crew member was likely still asleep, but when he woke, he'd have a fresh uniform to wear.

Before I could continue with the routine, the doors swished open, and Daila stormed inside. In her hand was a flat computer tablet. Interior lights from the uniform ward reflected off the LCD screen, and I couldn't read it.

"This is unacceptable," she said. She snapped the tablet into the universal port on the wall. The main computer lit up, and official documents filled the screen. My reassignment to security section was no longer secret.

"I was told to keep my work with security section confidential," I said. "I assumed you knew."

"I don't care about your assignment to security section. To be honest, I was waiting for you to move on. I've already met with TJ in personnel."

"Then I don't understand the problem," I said.

"The problem is this." She grabbed a laser pointer and aimed it at the screen. I turned and stared at the official paperwork. It was signed by both Neptune and Captain Katherine Ryder and stated the identity of the new uniform lieutenant on Moon Unit 6.

"Ensign" Pika.

21: REASSIGNMENT

THE LANGUAGE OF THE REASSIGNMENT paperwork was standard: *Reassignment of Ensign Pika to uniform ward effective immediately.* Additionally, a new chain of command had been established: *Ensign Pika to report to Lt. Sylvia Stryker during transition. All duties of uniform ward have been reassigned to security section.*

"I am in charge of uniforms," Daila said, tapping her chest for emphasis. "Me! I know you're behind this. You're coming for my job next, aren't you? I won't have it. I studied my butt off to graduate from the academy. If I hadn't broken my leg skiing, I would have been on Moon Unit 5, not you." Her fists were balled so tightly her skin stretched across her knuckles and turned white.

I'd mistakenly thought Daila's animosity toward me had to do with her history with

Neptune. And in a way, it did, but not for the reason I'd originally suspected. Daila's history with Neptune was water under the bridge. She didn't care about that.

She cared about me taking her place on the previous moon trek. Her brother had been killed on the ship and I'd been the one to find his body. In the uniform ward. Where he would have gone for one reason. He expected to find his sister there. He'd caught someone else in the act of sabotaging the ship, and that had led to him being killed. Left with nothing but misplaced anger, Daila blamed me for her brother's death.

There wasn't a darn thing I was going to say to make her see things differently. I had my own pain wrapped up in the memory of that trip, and I had no intention of reliving it. That's part of being a soldier, even if technically (up to five minutes ago) I was just a lieutenant in charge of uniforms. When push came to shove, I'd done what I'd studied my whole life to do: put the safety of the ship and its passengers in front of my own. And I'd do it again and again and again.

I gestured toward the screen. "Yeoman, have you confirmed the veracity of those documents with the captain?"

"Why? Are they fake?"

I radioed the bridge. "Uniform ward to the bridge. Requesting council with Captain Ryder."

"Captain Ryder here. Congratulations, Lieu-tenant. Stryker. It's a long-overdue assignment."

"And the uniform ward?"

"Neptune says you're fully capable of training Ensign Pika to oversee your original assignment."

My doubts were erased. Neptune *had* been listening in on my meeting with Anatol, and he had a plan.

This morning, after we revived Pika, Neptune had told me to fit her in an ensign uniform. He knew even then he was going to set this plan into action, before I met with Anatol, before I initiated the problem-with-the-ship report. I didn't know if it was sweet or diabolical how he made it happen when we needed it most. But the communication with the captain confirmed one thing: the assign-ment was legitimate.

"Neptune will outfit you with a regulation uniform for security section. In the meantime, show Ensign Pika the ropes."

"And Yeoman Teron?" I asked. "Will her responsibilities change further?"

"Yeoman Teron will receive specific instruc-tions from Commander Anatol."

"Thank you. Stryker out."

I released the computer tablet from the wall and handed it back to Daila. "This wasn't my call," I said.

"That doesn't make it right." She took the tablet and left.

Despite the paperwork and confirmation from the captain, I was surprised when Pika showed up for her assignment at Zulu Twenty-One. She was dressed in the uniform I'd altered and scrubbed clean of sparkles, which I mistakenly understood as her interest in her new job. But since Pika had exactly zero interest in learning how to be an effective uniform lieutenant, I wouldn't be leaving anytime soon.

Soiled uniforms dropped from the chute into the laundry bin, and I tried to show Pika how to fasten them onto the cleaning screens and insert the screens into the row of machines along the wall. Pika found it far more interesting to wait until my back was turned to pull every single uniform out of the inventory closet and make a pile in the middle of the carpet. You would think that would lead nicely into a lesson on how to fold and organize the uniforms.

You would have been mistaken. Like I was.

By the time the end of the shift arrived, I was convinced of one thing. Neptune had fixed it so I'd be doing two jobs, not one. Three if you counted Gremlon-sitting. I'd folded and returned every uniform to the closet and locked the closet so Pika couldn't get back in. Four of the five newly cleaned uniforms were standard regulation, so I added them to the closet as well. The fifth, a generously cut red shirt for our lead engineer, would require delivery to its owner. Ofra had already warned me of the expense of his custom uniforms. I suspected he'd appreciate the extra effort to make sure he got it back in pristine condition.

I logged out of the computer and powered off the inventory system. "Pika, let's go."

"Where?"

"To my room."

"Can I play with Cat?"

"Sure, if you're not too tired from work," I said sarcastically.

"No. I like work! It's fun, fun, fun!"

She skipped out the door and into the hallway. She appeared to have made a complete recovery from the attack earlier. I caught up with her and led the way to my quarters. I handed Cat to her, and Pika practically vibrated with excitement. She dropped onto my bed and chattered at the robot cat, who recognized her voice and responded. I was about to change into a non-regulation outfit when static filled my ear.

"Stryker. Security section."

"I'm tired. I want five minutes to sit down and relax."

"Now."

"Fine." I stood back up and attached my bubble

helmet to my uniform. "Pika, will you be okay here?"

"Yes, yes, yes!"

"Are you sure you don't want to go to your quarters?"

"I'm sure."

"Okay. If you get hungry, there's food in my suitcase. Just—try not to eat it all."

She smiled, showing me all fifty teeth. I had a very strong feeling my secret stash of food would be gone by the time I returned to my chambers. *If* I returned to my chambers. If I managed not to get arrested for lying to the chief science officer or faking an emergency or sneaking Zeke onto the ship.

Protecting my stash of comfort food was the least of my problems.

22: IN THE HEAT OF THE NIGHT

Neptune was waiting for me outside security section. "Why are you wearing your helmet?"

It felt like forever since the Martians had attacked me, and with everything now on my plate, the threat from the little green men was the last thing I wanted to think about. "I had a run-in with some Martians and let's just say I have a renewed appreciation for my oxygen supply and personal space."

"Did you tell someone? I didn't get a report."

"I haven't reported it yet."

"Go."

"Go where? We need to coordinate mission details before Zeke arrives, and Anatol plans to be on site, so we're going to have to come up with a cover. The Martians can wait."

"'Go' was a command for you to tell me what happened."

I thought of the Martian hands on me after I'd left Neptune's quarters. "I don't want to talk about it."

"I'm your supervisor, and I'm the head of security on this ship. If something on Moon Unit 6 represents a threat of any kind, I need to know."

"About that. You're head of security. Where's the rest of your crew? It can't just be you and now me."

"They're doing their jobs."

"How come I never see them?"

"That's part of their job."

"I see you all the time."

"That's different."

I was about to ask how but thought better of it. Maybe all this attention was considered training.

"Back to you," he said. "Failure to report a crime on the ship is a violation of section—"

"—four five two," we said at the same time. "I know," I added.

"If you know then stop stalling and make your verbal report."

"They ganged up on me, okay? The Martians tripped me and shoved an inhaler into my mouth to incapacitate me. I was face down on the carpet, and they dragged me into an empty room. The male Venusian, Synn, scared them off."

"Venusians aren't known for interrupting—" Neptune didn't finish that thought. "As I said, the whole planet is turbocharged. Whatever the Martians were doing to you would have seemed completely normal to a Venusian."

"That's totally creepy. You know that, right? I don't think the Martians knew Synn was going to look the other way, and since he's twice their height, they scattered and left me there. But I think he would have just stood there and watched." I shuddered.

"You're dull."

"I'm not dull. I'm conventional. I have no interest in a group of horny green Martians."

He pointed at my hand. "Your skin."

I looked down. In the low light of security section, my hands didn't look any different from how they usually looked. "Your face," he said. "It's pale. Are you sure you're okay?"

"I'm fine," I said.

Neptune walked toward me. He put both hands on my bubble helmet and twisted to free it from the grooves on my uniform. A rush of warmth washed over me, and a purplish glow cast onto the back of the mainframe computer.

Neptune put his finger under my chin and tipped my head back. I was looking directly at him. Our bodies were inches apart. Waves of heat cascaded off him. My thoughts swirled like dust particles around an astronaut's boots after stepping onto a lunar surface. *Protect the ship. Don't drop your guard. Show no weakness.* And the counter-thought that Neptune was going to kiss me, and it had been a really long time since I'd been kissed or even wanted to kiss someone like I wanted to kiss Neptune, and that maybe security section would be slightly more comfortable if I took off my restrictive layer of Stealthyester®. I pulled Neptune toward me. He put his hands on my arms. And then something clicked in my mind.

"That's it," I said. "That's how we do it."

Neptune raised one eyebrow.

I stepped away from him. "You have to be with me at the rocket nozzle. You get hot around me. I get hot around you." I waved my hands quickly to dismiss the possible-other meaning of my words. "Not hot-hot. Temperature hot. If we stand next to each other close enough to the beryllium spheres, Anatol's diagnostic devices won't be able to tell where the heat is coming from. It'll confirm my report about the fire we picked up from the comet, and the potential threat if the spheres overheat."

Neptune watched me closely. There was enough space between us for me to realize his intense stare had nothing to do with wanting to kiss me and everything to do with what I said. He was listening to my mission. He was giving me the respect one security officer would give another.

Unless he'd already worked all that out and had been waiting for me to catch up.

"You already thought of this, didn't you?" I asked. "From when I was in your quarters. You knew what would happen from your time on Venus, and you were testing me to see if we could create the kind of reaction that we could use in a mission. Right?"

"As a security officer, it's your job to identify threats, weaknesses, and unique opportunities. The effects of Venus on your Plunian makeup create a unique opportunity."

"How come it's not a threat to the captain? She's Plunian too. She's not walking around all charged up." I turned away from Neptune and stared at my bubble helmet. A smudge had appeared on the surface, and I used the edge of my sleeve to buff it out. "It's the helmet, isn't it? That's why she wears her helmet all the time. It's not about the oxygen for her; it's about keeping a barrier between her and other people on the ship. She probably regulates her temperature too. That's how she stays in control."

"That's part of it."

"And what else?"

Neptune crossed his arms over his chest. "Your friend said you glowed when you said my name."

"You weren't supposed to remember that." He raised both eyebrows. "You're the first person who ever treated me as an equal. When our last moon trek was over, you recognized I was qualified to be a security officer. When my dad was arrested, everybody turned their backs on me. It wasn't like I had a lot of options. I moved home to help my mom in the dry ice mines, but other than that, I was pretty much on my own."

"What about Vaan Marshall?"

Vaan was the youngest member of Federation Council. He was also my first real boyfriend. When we attended the academy together, it had seemed like we were destined to become one of the power couples of the universe: him in politics, and me in security. But after he was drafted into the council and the council voted to banish my dad to Colony 13, Vaan and I broke up. Just because he'd recused himself from the vote didn't mean I would forgive him. In my world, there were loyalties that ran deeper than politics. Vaan and I hadn't seen eye to eye on that.

Whether it was because Vaan wanted a second chance with me or to further his political career, he'd initiated proceedings against Neptune for actions on Moon Trek 5. There were enough crew members who could testify on Neptune's behalf, and Vaan knew that, but he'd followed protocol all the same. If the charges against Neptune stood, he could be arrested. I shook the thoughts away involuntarily. I didn't want to think about that.

"Stryker."

I shifted my attention back to Neptune. "Vaan's Plunian too. All Plunian, not half Plunian like me. So yes, there was a time when I was with Vaan, but that ended when my dad was arrested."

"And Zeke Champion?"

I put my hands on my hips. "What is this? An interrogation into my love life? We're supposed to be designing a mission. A mission I'm only participating in to save your hide. And Zeke is too. So maybe you should get over yourself and focus on that and not who makes me hot." Instantly I regretted the choice of words. "Warm." Not that much better. "Bright."

Neptune stared at me for a few beats, and then spoke. "For your plan to work, you need to assess and understand the variables. If you get—bright—around me and not Champion, then we can proceed. Do you—get bright—around him?"

"No."

"Do you—get bright—around anybody on this ship?"

I dropped my eyes from his face to his chest, and then, remembering how important it was to show no weakness, forced myself to look back at his face. "Just you."

"Good. Now you understand the variables. Now you can design a mission."

23: COVERT OPS

"You want me to design the mission?" I asked. "You know more than I do. I just assumed you'd be in charge."

"You assumed wrong. I'm too close to it. You're an official member of Moon Unit 6 security team. Planning missions is part of your job."

"Yes, but I've been a member of the team for less than a day. Are you sure there isn't some kind of orientation I need to complete first?"

"Quit stalling."

This was what I'd wanted my whole life, and here it was. Being handed to me. And as scary as the challenge and the possible outcomes were if something went wrong, I knew I could do this.

"Anatol expects me in the rocket nozzle at Zulu Four," I said. "He issued the work order for Zeke's drones. The ship will enter the asteroid minefield and go on autopilot. You need to be in the rocket nozzle for some other reason."

"Security."

"I'm security. You won't need to be there too."

"You've only been in security for a few hours," Neptune said. "It would be highly questionable for me to allow you to oversee something of this magnitude without supervision. As chief science officer of the ship, Anatol expects that."

"How do you know?"

"When I heard of his plan to recommend a reassignment to the captain, I demanded a meeting. He communicated details of your Council Chambers conversation to me and explained his rationale. Standard procedure."

"But you probably already knew whatever he told you because you were listening in on the comm device, right? Why'd you need to demand a meeting?"

"Anatol recommended the promotion as a test. If your plan was a cover for something else, he needed to know who you were working with or if you were working independently. As second officer, he has the power to reassign personnel without following protocol, which he did."

"He gave me a fake promotion to trap you."

"Nobody questioned your ability to do the job he assigned you, and your promotion will stand when the mission is complete. If Anatol assigned someone to my team and I didn't question it, he would have suspected us both."

I leaned back against Neptune's desk. "Let me get this straight. I convinced him we need a fleet of drones to cool the beryllium spheres while we're in the minefield as a cover story to open the hatch and get Zeke on board. Anatol didn't even question my report. He gave me a promotion and invited me to watch so he could see who I told and whether or not I had a different agenda?"

"Yes. Now follow that train of thought and tell me what Anatol is going to do next."

"He promoted me to your team without advising you. You would have challenged his decision except you'd have no choice, right?" He raised one eyebrow. "I mean, we both know I'm qualified, and you're extremely lucky to have me on your team, but still, you have a reputation for wanting to be in control and him going over your head probably made you mad."

"He's a senior officer. My feelings toward his decision play no role in this scenario." Neptune picked a space blaster off the charging station next to his desk and attached it to his belt.

"But you pressed him on the mission and said you need to be there when the drones arrive. Was that smart? Now we're both tied up with Anatol. Who's going to open the hatch for Zeke?"

"There is no way the head of security would

allow a recently promoted member of his team proximity to the beryllium spheres unsupervised. It is too big of a threat to the ship."

"So when Anatol invited me, everything changed. You had to be there."

"No. If you had turned down the offer, I would have gone instead. You would have let Zeke in."

"You're saying it's my fault?"

"I'm saying Anatol knows more than he's letting on. Be careful around him, Stryker. It's possible he has his own agenda."

There wasn't much more for Neptune and me to discuss, and with the silent agreement that we needed to turn up the heat (so to speak) around the beryllium spheres to fake out Anatol, the best plan was to go our separate ways. I re-secured my helmet before leaving security section and kept to the main corridors. We were less than seven hours from the mission, and despite Neptune's strong suggestion that I take the HVPTS to avoid any unexpected threats, I wasn't risking my equilibrium anytime in the foreseeable future.

I needed to be at the top of my game, and that meant eating and sleeping before convening at the rocket nozzle. Instead of going to my quarters where I'd end up bunking with Pika, I headed to the cafeteria for food.

The crew cafeteria was an octagonal room with vending machines on the perimeter and groupings of tables and chairs in the center. For all the bells and whistles that had been incorporated into the passenger areas of the ship, the caf was what it was: a utilitarian dining room for the non-ranking masses. Until a few hours ago, that was me. For now, it seemed wise to keep my new assignment to myself.

Since last night was First Dinner, tonight was the night when crew members were rotated through open tables at the Space Bar. Moon Unit Corporation had assigned each hire a number and numbers were called as tables were available. By the end of the trek, when the novelty of dressing for dinner paled in comparison to hanging out with friends in lounging attire, numbers came up with more frequency. Between the vacancies in the restaurant and the illness caused by tainted protein packs in the vending machines, the cafeteria was mostly unoccupied.

I scanned my identification card and selected synthetic pasta with cryogenic clam sauce. It was a far cry from the dinner I'd had at the captain's table. Just as I was about to pack it all into a sealed meal transport wrapper, I spotted a familiar face eating alone at the table in the corner and thought twice about my plan to eat in my room. It was Lumiere, the Independent Border Patrol officer. Maybe this wasn't so different from First Dinner after all? The presence of IBP on board Moon Unit

6 made a lot more sense with the knowledge that Xina was a an escaped convict with a tracking chip in her head.

And now that I was officially a part of the security team, it seemed prudent to take advantage of the opportunity to find out exactly how much Officer Lumiere knew.

24: DINNER DATE

"Do you mind if I join you?" I asked Lumiere.

"Please do," he said, gesturing toward an open chair. "Once people hear I'm IBP, they tend to steer clear of me."

I shrugged. "Once people hear my dad was arrested for collusion with space pirates, they steer clear of me too."

Lumiere didn't react, which in a way meant he passed my impromptu test. I had assumed he knew about my dad. Most of the crew had, and IBP would have had access to more believable channels than gossip.

I took off my helmet and set it on a vacant chair. The border patrol agent took a long drink of his green beverage. "I heard about you," he said, confirming my suspicions. "Before I took the assignment. Moon Unit turned their crew manifests over to IBP for background checks. Sorry about what happened to Plunia. Must have been difficult."

"To be honest, I don't think I've fully processed the fact that my entire planet is gone. I miss my mom, but she and I always talked about how I'd be on my own if I ever landed a job on a spaceship. This was my dream from when I was a kid. So even though I know what happened, I still feel like she's with me."

"And your dad?"

"What Jack Stryker did and what happens to him now aren't my concern."

Lumiere nodded as if he understood. I hadn't expected to blurt out my feelings for my father, but it was unexpectedly easy to talk to Lumiere. Maybe because he admitted to already knowing my past.

"What about you? What's your story?" I asked.

He looked at me sideways.

"Come on," I said. "We're in the crew cafeteria. For the next five minutes, pretend you're off-duty and let's talk like normal people."

He cocked his head to the side, appeared to consider what I asked, and then shrugged as if giving in to the suggestion. "Born on Mars to a second-generation couple from Earth. Dad worked as an alien bounty hunter. Mom did the books."

"Where are they now?"

"They passed away a few years ago. Sabotage of the air unit wiped out their whole neighborhood."

"Where were you?"

"I was part of a team that worked on star charts. We were on a mission. I didn't find out what happened until I got home months later."

"How'd you go from star charts to border patrol?"

He picked up his fork and pushed the remaining few nutrition pellets to the side of his plate. "Mapping stars didn't seem nearly as important after I found out the air unit was sabotaged. I wanted someone to pay. I made a nuisance of myself to the investigators, and they banished me to Colony 13 while they completed their reports. When my time was over, I found out they filed the report with incomplete data, and nobody was held accountable. I couldn't live with that, so I signed up for Independent Space Patrol."

"Is Border Patrol a division of Space Patrol?"

He nodded. "I took the jobs that opened up, but I always suspected someone who wasn't supposed to be on Mars was responsible for the sabotage. When a position became available in border patrol, I went for it. I've been doing the job for the past twelve years."

"And? Have you had any luck finding the person responsible for the sabotage?"

He shook his head. "When I started, that was

the most important thing. Now that I've been doing the job for a while, I see how many crimes are committed. I have a better understanding of my role in the big picture. Letting my personal agenda override my responsibilities would not only be reckless, but it would put countless law-abiding citizens at risk."

For the next few minutes, we ate in silence. I couldn't help comparing Lumiere's attitude toward his job with Neptune's mission to rescue his sister and make a deal with an escaped convict to do so. Neptune said his actions were inspired by what had happened to me. Yet comparatively speaking, Lumiere's and my backgrounds were more similar. Both of us lost our parents through circumstances we couldn't control. Both of us had to accept that someone else's agenda had destroyed the lives we knew. At school, I was taught the importance of following the rules, but once I dropped out, I quickly learned how important it was to know when to break them too. I wasn't 100 percent sure where the line was between acceptable rule breaking and reckless rule breaking, but I'd recognize it when I saw it.

I hoped.

"You said Moon Unit Corporation turned over all the crew manifests for background checks. I'm guessing they thoroughly vetted the passengers too. What is it you're looking for?"

Lumiere's looked at me sideways again.

I set down my fork and held up my hands. "I'm not asking you to tell me anything you can't. I'm just curious. Assuming everybody on this ship was checked out—and that's probably a pretty good assumption considering what happened on the last Moon Unit—it seems unusual for them to bring you on board. Passengers might get concerned if they suspect you're after someone because the only people you'd be after are bad ones. Right?"

"Moon Unit Corp has a lot to lose if something goes wrong on this trip. They contracted with me to cross their T's and dot their I's."

"You're like security to watch over security. You're just making sure everything goes as planned, and in case it turns out someone on Moon Unit 6 is doing something to jeopardize the success of the trip, you're already here. You can step in and take control of things."

"Something like that."

I looked over one shoulder and then the other, making sure we weren't being eavesdropped upon. The cafeteria was mostly empty, and the only company we had were two off-duty navigators playing a friendly game of Ping Pong at the far side of the room. The steady bounce-*whap*, bounce-*whap* of the hollow ball and rubberized paddles was white noise, blending in with the constant hum of the vending machines and the occasional rumble of dry ice in the refrigeration unit.

"The last Moon Unit had a member of Federation Council on board for the same reason," I said. "Vaan Marshall. I'm surprised the company didn't make the same arrangements."

"Commander Marshall has been busy with the Plunian Relief Effort. You didn't know?"

"No." My stomach turned.

"Surprising. He listed you as one of the recipients of the fund. You were supposed to be contacted with an allotment and a start-up kitty to rebuild your life. Didn't anyone tell you?"

"Who would have told me? I didn't keep in touch with anyone when Moon Unit 5 mission ended."

"Neptune knew. He didn't say anything?"

"No. Are you sure?"

Lumiere nodded. "Neptune doesn't do anything without a reason. You'd best watch yourself around him until you know what he wants."

I already knew what he wanted. What I didn't know was what he was willing to sacrifice to get it— and if that sacrifice included my life.

25: MANIPULATED?

ASIDE FROM THE HUNGER THAT THREATENED to distract me from the issues at hand (and the issue count was rapidly mounting), I recognized two things. One: this was the second time I'd learned something unexpected about Neptune. The first was when his name turned up in the transcripts of incarcerated-for-life space pirate Cheung Qidd. I hadn't confronted him about that yet because I didn't know what it meant. But this new intel, that Neptune knew Vaan had Federation Council funding for me to set up a new life but hadn't cooperated in letting Vaan know where to find me—that was something else. Neptune wouldn't do something like that to be rude. He was security. He'd follow protocol, give Vaan the coordinates for where I was, and go on with his life.

But he hadn't, and that meant he had a reason for me not to get that money. I had to find out why.

The second thing I couldn't shake was the knowledge that Lumiere had run checks on every person and alien on board the ship. Specifically, he had background checks on Neptune and Xina. Neptune said he'd faked Xina's data to get her on board the ship, but what if Lumiere knew Xina wasn't who she said she was, and he was biding his time, waiting to find out what her—and Neptune's —end game was and use the knowledge for his own gain?

Either way, I had to access those files and get some answers for myself.

One thing stood between me and those answers: Lumiere. Regardless of the missions that were stacking up come Zulu Four, I had a new one to fit in before then. Access Lumiere's IBP database.

It wasn't lost on me that Lumiere would also have access to the sealed criminal files we were trying to keep quiet. He probably trusted whatever had come back from the initial background check on Xina when she won the contest, but what Zeke had uploaded wouldn't match. And Zeke, Neptune, and I knew if Xina's records were given anything more than a cursory glance, the fake Venusian would be exposed for what she was (or wasn't).

Sating my hunger proved to be a good enough reason why I stopped my side of the conversation. The food perked me up, and when I finished everything I'd taken from the vending machines, I looked longingly at the chocolate dessert on Lumiere's tray.

"Take it," he said. "I'm full, and if you don't eat it, it's going into the trash."

"It would be a shame to put that in the trash," I said. "What's in it?"

"I'm pretty sure it's 100 percent sugar." He picked up the dessert and set it in front of me. My hand rested on my spoon, and his fingers brushed over mine. The gesture struck me as interesting. When I'd first encountered Lumiere in OB One before our departure, he hadn't shown the smallest hint of being attracted to me. He'd been slightly more attentive at First Dinner, but I'd written that off to his surprise that I was at the captain's table. And here we were, in the crew cafeteria, and I was reasonably sure his lingering touch was on purpose. It backed up Neptune's intel that Moon Unit 6's proximity to Venus brought out a heightened desire for contact between crew members. A fact confirmed a moment later when Lumiere curled his fingers around mine and gently rubbed his thumb back and forth over the back of my hand.

Whatever the trigger, Lumiere was distracted by more than his food. And our small talk had made me comfortable enough to relax for the first time since I'd found Xina's body.

"Lumiere," I said softly, "The closer we get to Venus, the more pleasant the atmosphere becomes. Don't you think?"

"Venus does make things more pleasant," he said. "I never noticed how pretty your coloring was."

Crap. I was probably starting to glow. It was bad enough when it happened around Neptune, but if I glowed around other members of the crew, not only would I get a bad reputation, but I wouldn't be able to use my chemistry with Neptune to distract Anatol. Without realizing it, I pulled my hand away from Lumiere's and dropped it into my lap where I balled it up with the other hand. Lumiere's naked disappointment embarrassed me, and I looked down for no reason other than I needed to see the extent of the problem.

Which was when I discovered that I wasn't glowing. My skin was its usual shade of lavender. Lumiere's touch hadn't affected me in the least.

Like Neptune said, once I understood the variables, I could use them. And I could use this.

26: LOVE IS IN THE AIR

As soon as I realized Lumiere felt emotions I didn't, I recognized the opportunity for what it was. My window to steal his files and get answers for myself.

"Do you want to get out of here?" I asked him. His disappointment vanished. "Maybe go to your quarters?" I added.

"Yes," he said. He pushed his chair backward and grabbed both of our trays. I watched the dessert go into the trash bin. It was for the best. The dessert would have caused a blood sugar spike and crash within hours and made it more difficult to be on my game come go-time. And now, I had a whole other mission to complete before then.

A buzz of static crackled in my ear. Assuming Zeke was in a repair pod on his way to the intercept point, the crackle was Neptune. I didn't want him listening in or knowing what I was up to. I tore a corner off my napkin, rolled the paper between my palms, and pressed it into my ear like a plug.

When I first inserted the comm device, I discovered I couldn't get it back out. Zeke had fun after he found the frequency, but soon the bigger challenge turned into shutting it off. After careful experimentation, Zeke came up with two possible fixes: a temporary earplug or an electrical current fed into my auditory canal. With only a 74 percent success rate on the second choice, my decision was easy. That night I started wearing ear plugs daily until I got the call for Moon Unit 6. That was why Neptune didn't know I was going to be on the ship.

Eliminating any chance of Neptune hearing what I was about to do made me slightly more comfortable with my plan.

Lumiere and I left the cafeteria. Though I wanted to put on my bubble helmet, it probably would have sent out a red flag to the man I was pretending to seduce. We walked side by side through the corridors until we reached the end unit in Sector 3. He waved his keycard over the sensor, and the door slid open.

I hesitated for a moment. What if I couldn't distract him? What if I couldn't get away before Zulu Four? What if the entire mission went awry because I had the bright idea to try to steal computer files to uncover the real reason a border patrol officer was on the ship? I couldn't risk it—not any of it. Plan B.

Lumiere's quarters were more along the line of what I would have expected a ranking officer to have than the gray of Neptune's room. Instead of a bed that folded down from the wall for use or a cot, Lumiere's was a clear, inflatable mattress covered in satin sheets.

I thought it best not to spend too much time staring at the bed, so I turned my back on it and assessed the rest of the room while determining my next course of action. In addition to the chairs in the center of the room and digital library for reading pleasure along the back wall. Objects were tied down with bindings, typical for those uncomfortable with their belongings floating around when the gravity was switched off. I noticed one thing more important than Lumiere's furniture and collection of books: a sizeable bar filled with a wider selection of aperitifs than existed anywhere outside the bar at Ion 54.

I learned a lot during my time at the space academy, but my education didn't stop when I dropped out. It didn't follow the usual sanctioned lesson plan, either. I'd learned enough by that point to know that the enemy often didn't play fair. Somewhere around then, I saw the benefit of thinking like the enemy. In addition to the time I spent tinkering with broken electronics for spending money and helping mom in the dry ice mines, I befriended a local mixologist and studied toxicology.

Security officers were required to be on their game at all times. It was one of the reasons my need for pure oxygen caused me to fail the physical on the previous moon trek. If we couldn't operate at top levels, then we couldn't be relied upon, period. What they didn't teach at the academy was that we could mix minerals and beverage strains from various planets into tailor-made combinations that would incapacitate anybody. That's where profiling came in handy. By determining a person's genetic makeup, I could put together the most effective combination.

It was easy enough to profile me as Plunian—I was purple. The Martians would have known about my need for oxygen, and by forcing me to inhale something else, they knew I'd be out of commission. I could just as easily profile them because they were little and green. But others on the ship weren't so easy, and Lumiere was one of them. I could ask him and come up with a profile on the fly, or I could go with the tried and true and slip him a Methanol Intoxicant Cocktail—known in certain circles as a Mickey.

I set my helmet on his table next to a game of chess under a clear dome. "Can I fix you a drink?"

"I was going to open a bottle of Saturnian wine," he said. "I brought one for special occasions."

I turned around. Lumiere had a bottle of wine in one hand and two stemless glasses in the other. No doubt he could handle his wine; otherwise, he wouldn't even suggest it.

I smiled in a way that I hoped was enchanting. Lumiere's eyes darkened. Okay, maybe too enchanting. How close to Venus were we?

"My skills go beyond uniform management," I said. "How about you make yourself comfortable and let me spoil you."

"Sure," he said. He sat on the corner of the bed and pulled off his boots, turned around and pulled his white shirt off over his head and covered his bare torso with a lounging jacket that fastened at the waist. Lumiere was moving fairly fast, which meant I was going to have to step up the pace or I'd be in real trouble. Martians-in-the-hallway trouble. I shuddered.

"Are you cold?" he asked.

"No," I said quickly. "That's one of the side effects of being part Plunian. Our body temperature runs hotter than earthlings. If I had my way, the whole ship would be twenty degrees cooler."

I turned my back on Lumiere and scanned the

bottles on his cart. A Quick Mickey would do the trick, and I knew how to make one fast, but Lumiere's bottles didn't have labels. "You have a fully stocked bar," I said.

"I like to entertain. Work hard and play hard, right?"

That was a pretty good attitude for what I had coming. I unlocked the cabinet and pulled out a bottle with clear blue liquid, poured it into a glass and added in splashes of pink and purple liquids, and dropped in four sugar cubes to activate it. While I jiggled the glass, I looked over my shoulder.

At Lumiere's feet.

I looked up. He floated in mid-air. "I turned the gravity off." He grinned and held out my helmet, which had floated off the table. I took it and set it underneath. "That'll make things more fun, don't you think?"

"Um, sure. Here," I glanced at the glass in my hand. The liquid rose out of the glass and into the air. I moved the glass up quickly and corralled the fluid, and then put my hand on top and held the drink up to him. "You better drink this fast. I'll make another one and join you."

While Lumiere poured the contents of his drink down his throat, I pretended to mix up my own cocktail. I sipped from an empty glass, put it into the cabinet, and dropped into a chair. I took my time unzipping my left boot, and looked up, prepared to make an excuse about the zipper being stuck, when I saw the one thing any other woman in my situation would have hated to see. Lumiere had fallen asleep in midair.

Our "date" was officially over.

27: OFRA STARR

I DIDN'T WASTE TIME PULLING MY BOOT BACK on. While Lumiere floated in the air above me, I ran an assessing gaze around the perimeter of his quarters until I found what I was looking for.

Independent Border Patrol wasn't a regulation crew position on Moon Unit 6, but Space Patrol was an important enough policing body in the galaxy that when they requested a room on a spaceship, they got one of the rooms reserved for visiting officers. His computer was mounted to the wall just like mine was in uniform ward. That would save me time.

My newly acquired security credentials would save me time too. I wonder how Neptune would feel knowing I was about to use them against him.

I zipped my gravity boot and activated the computer. I had no idea how long Lumiere was going to be out, and not only did I need to get information, I needed to get the heck out of there before he woke. Things would be awkward the next time I saw him, but I'd deal with that then.

Once the computer was up and running, I bypassed the main menu to the files, did a search for "Stryker" to figure out his filing system, and then applied his file naming convention to Xina and Neptune. The files were zipped, but I could easily break into them on my own time. I forwarded copies of both files to my computer in a zipped folder named "Care Instructions for Stealthyester®," closed out of the windows, erased the data log, and powered off.

The whole thing took me seventeen seconds.

I turned around to find Lumiere shifting his position. If you've never seen someone sleep in zero gravity, trust me, it's an odd sight. Chances were when he woke, he'd forget all about our rendezvous and sleep off the effects of the drink. Which would work out extra great for me, but I wasn't going to stick around any longer than I had to just in case. I ducked under his floating body, grabbed my helmet, and left.

It was a little after Zulu Twenty-Two. I hurried to the stairs, arriving at the uniform ward a few minutes later.

Unfortunately, I wasn't the only one.

Ofra Starr, the flamboyant engineer with a

penchant for glittery cosmetics, towered over Pika. It appeared she was having her first encounter with him. From the looks of it, Pika hadn't done a whole lot to fulfill her job duties on her own.

"Ofra, isn't it a little late for you to be hanging around the uniform ward?" I asked.

He turned to face me. "Tell me this isn't true. I cannot trust my custom uniform to a Gremlon. I can't. Do you know how many tailors I had to interview to find one who knew how to make French seams? This whole galaxy is going to pot. Where are the tradespeople who take pride in their work? Do I have to go to Uranus to find skilled craftsmen? Is that what this has come to?"

"Mr. Starr, I washed your uniform," Pika said. "I ran it through the machine and everything."

"Tell me you did not." He put the back of his hand up to his forehead. "Lieutenant Stryker, tell me this wee pink thing did not run a custom uniform through the machines. If you did, I just—I can't. There are no words. No words." He held both hands up in front of him, fingers splayed, eyes rolled up. Ofra tended to be a little dramatic.

"Pika was appointed to the uniform ward earlier today. We spent the day in training, but it's a lot to take in, especially for a Gremlon." I looked at Pika and smiled. Her ears flattened against her head, and her eyes got big. I shifted my attention back to Ofra. "I was here when your uniform came in, and I recognized it immediately. I took special care with it."

"You did?" he asked. He dabbed the back of his hand on his forehead as if blotting off perspiration, but the hallway was cool enough that I suspected the gesture was more for effect than practicality. "You're a saint, darling."

"There's just one problem," I said. "It's after hours, and if the three of us enter the ward to get your uniform, it's going to send a notification to the bridge. I don't think any of us want them investigating what kind of crisis require us to log in after hours. You did bring a spare uniform, didn't you? We were told to show up with two clean uniforms."

"Of course, I did. But there's a small child running around this ship. Did you know that? Why would parents bring a *child* on a trip to *Venus*? For *fun*?" He shuddered not unlike how I'd shuddered in Lumiere's quarters. "Perish the thought." He untied the belt on his custom pink velvet lounging jacket and showed me a purple stain on his uniform just above the Moon Unit insignia.

I smiled. "Welcome to the club. I have a lime green stain on my evening gown from First Dinner."

"You don't."

"I do."

He leaned in. "Young Ellison is trouble. We must plot revenge of the highest order."

"I'm in. Let me know your plan."

Ofra stood straight and reknotted his belt. He looked at Pika, who had her head down but her eyes up, openly admiring the engineer from under her lashes.

"You're sparkly," Pika said. She batted her eyelashes a few times. " I like things that are sparkly."

"I tell you what," I said. "How about I send your uniform through tube delivery? It should be at your quarters later this evening."

"I suppose that would work," he said dismissively.

"In the meantime, Pika, why don't you escort your new friend to his quarters?"

"Okay, okay, okay," she said in a soft, girlish voice.

"She is a dear, isn't she?" He put his fingertips under her chin and tipped her head back. "And those lashes! What I wouldn't give for lashes like that." Pika grinned, flashing all fifty of her teeth. "Magnificent," he added. "Okay, my dear, you're forgiven."

Pika had the good sense to bat her eyelashes a few more times.

I sent the two of them on their way and went the opposite direction. I hid around the corner until I was sure they were gone from the hallway and returned. I hadn't been lying about a notification being sent to the bridge if the three of us entered, but with my credentials from security sector, and my original assignment to be right where I was, my presence wasn't particularly suspicious.

Besides, I only needed a minute or two.

I entered the uniform ward, placed my hand on the touchpad and accessed the zip files. The first thing I did was make a copy and send it to Cat's coordinates. Which turned out to be a very good instinct because seconds after the file was sent, I detected Daila standing in the shadows.

28: COLD AS ICE

"Yeoman Teron, what are you doing here?" I asked.

"I already told you I'd be conducting unannounced checks of the uniform ward. The condition here is deplorable. I've a mind to report Ensign Pika."

"The uniform ward isn't your responsibility anymore."

Daila looked angry. "Why are you here, Lieutenant Stryker? Can't the Gremlon do her job?"

I didn't much care if she reported me, but she didn't have to know that. "The BOP states that all crew members appear in uniform. One of the engineers is at risk of violating that protocol and needs his uniform cleaned immediately. Ensign Pika has not yet been trained on the sanitation machines, so I came here to handle the uniform myself."

I opened the steamer and removed Ofra's uniform. If there was any question about my story, the unique dimensions of the engineer's custom shirt answered them. I carried the newly cleaned uniform back to the center console. It took three unsuccessful attempts to fit it into the cylinder tube for delivery before I gave up. Had Pika remained with me, I could have tasked her to deliver it, but Neptune would have blown a gasket if he discovered us both there after hours.

Crap. Neptune. I'd forgotten all about the wad of napkin in my ear canal. He didn't know where I was or what I was up to. Which was good, except it wasn't. He was my boss now. Regardless of what I would learn when I read his files, he was responsible for my actions, and we were hours away from a very important covert mission. I was too smart to jeopardize the ship or the mission by acting recklessly or in renegade fashion. I tipped my head to the side and pulled the wad of napkin out of my ear.

A deafening frequency filled my head. I dropped Ofra's shirt and the delivery tube and fell to my knees. I must have yelled, though the high-pitched noise caused by the comm device affected my hearing.

Daila came out of the shadows and helped me up. She guided me to the bench along the far wall—

the same one I'd tried to sleep on earlier today. My equilibrium was off even more than it had been after multiple trips on the HVPTS and I was happy to sit, even though I knew there was precious little time to waste.

Daila swiped her passkey over the medical cabinet and pulled out an injection gun. She said something, jammed the injection point of the gun against the side of my neck and fired. I flinched. An icy cold sensation snaked through my system, down my arms, into my chest, and through my legs. The shivering started next. With quivering arms, I slowly brought my limbs in tight against my body to warm myself. I looked up at Daila. She stood a foot away from me, with the gun still in her hand, dangling from her side. She looked terrified.

"C-c-c-c-c-old," I stammered.

She dropped the gun on the carpet and reached for the emergency supply closet on the wall. Once opened, a silent alarm would trip and sound on the bridge and in Medi-Bay. An audible alarm would sound throughout the ship ten minutes later. Both were fail-safe measures in the event of an unforeseen emergency. With what Neptune and I had planned for later, I couldn't risk it.

"N-n-n-n-o," I said. My eyes moved down to Ofra's uniform on the floor. Daila snatched it from the carpet and pulled it on over my head. I fed my arms through the oversized sleeves slowly and then wrapped the extra fabric around me. I turned my head toward the uniform closet. "in-n-n-n-ventor-r-r-r-y." She ran to the closet, yanked it open, and grabbed an armful of uniforms that she dumped on top of me. I curled into a ball and closed my eyes and concentrated everything I had on generating heat from within.

Remember yesterday when I woke in midair? I would have given anything to replicate that. Because this time when I woke up, I was in the morgue. On the bright side, I was alive, which was more than I could say for the body next to me.

Even with her skin the color of steel, made more unflattering by the blue lights of the morgue, I recognized her. It was Xina.

But why was I laying on a cart next to Xina's cold, dead body?

The door swished open, and Doc entered. "Sylvia," he said. "You're alive."

"I would like to think so," I said.

"Yeoman Teron wasn't sure. She said you exhibited signs of extreme vertigo. She followed basic training measures and injected you with a high dose of Anti-Vert."

I put my hand on the side of my neck. Yes, it was all coming back to me. "I eat Anti-Vert pops all the time," I said. Doc raised his eyebrows, and they looked like pictures I'd seen of an open drawbridge, the space between them being where a ship would pass through. "Not all the time, but sometimes, if I'm in an environment that's low on oxygen, my equilibrium gets affected. Anti-Vert pops help."

"Yes, I imagine they do. In addition to the medicine they contain, there's a sizeable amount of crystalized oxygen in them."

"What happened?"

"Yeoman Teron's report states that she injected you, you collapsed, and your body temperature dropped to unusually dangerous levels. When her attempts to warm you with coverings didn't work, she contacted Medi-Bay, and we retrieved you."

Up to a point, the narrative sounded familiar. I glanced down at my body and saw Ofra's oversized, custom red shirt hanging off me. Not only was it wrinkled beyond measure, but it had gotten wet. Ofra was not going to be pleased, and frankly, I wasn't either. There was definitely something off-putting about being in Medi-Morgue of a spaceship while wearing a red shirt.

"I'm wet," I said.

"We submerged you in liquid goop to stabilize your core temperature."

"Goop?"

Doc smiled. "It's a non-toxic liquid gel that conducts heat without danger of burning. Glycol oxyoxynoic phosphate. I didn't think you'd require the technical term."

"Goop," I repeated. "My new favorite thing."

"Well, yes, it did do what we hoped, and it did it in a relatively short amount of time. Considering your condition, I didn't expect you to wake up until tomorrow."

"Why am I in the morgue?"

He pointed over his shoulder. "Medi-Bay is filled with sick crew members. Darn assembly crew didn't have the vending machines properly grounded, and the protein packs went bad again. The whole communications crew has been down."

"You've got a Medi-Bay filled with Martians?"

"Yep. That's what they get for traveling in a pack. For now, you just lay back down and rest."

"That's not necessary. I feel fine."

"Lieutenant Stryker, when you're under my care, you follow my rules. And right now, I'm telling you that you're not going anywhere until I give you the all-clear, and I don't plan to give you the all clear for at least twenty-four hours."

"But—"

"No buts. The captain knows you're under my care."

"What about Commander Anatol?"

Doc's brows dropped low over his eyes, making me a little nervous about asking any more questions. "How about instead of you asking questions, you answer one for me?"

"Sure," I said slowly.

He picked up a clear specimen jar from a shelf next to Xina's body. Inside was a small black disc suspended in gel. He pointed to the jar. "Do you want to tell me how you came to have a black ops communication device misfire in your ear canal?"

29: MEDI-MORGUE

THE NUMBER OF PROBLEMS FACING ME WAS quickly mounting. Doc's knowledge of the comm device was bad enough, but Neptune not being able to communicate with me, tonight of all nights, was worse. I had no idea where Neptune had gotten the comm or who Doc would tell about it. All I knew was that right now I was on my own.

I needed time to formulate a plan, but there wasn't any time. Except, if Doc was going to monitor me for the next twenty-four hours, the only thing I had was time.

I focused all my attention on Doc. It was a trick I'd learned at the academy. Zero in on one thing. The intensity of focus would hide any indicators of distractions and any side panic over my ever-growing list of promises, obligations, and secrets.

There was only one problem right now. Everything else faded into the background.

"Permission to speak freely?"

"I'm a doctor. You don't need to hide behind rank and order mumbo jumbo when you talk to me."

"Can anybody hear us?"

Doc agitated the jar with the comm device, and it remained suspended in the thick, gel-like substance. "Doubt it."

I closed my eyes for a moment, then opened them. The realization that the only person who would hear what I said was in the room with me was more freeing than I could have predicted. "In the break between moon treks, I participated in a privately funded program to test the range on new spec equipment. The conditions were complete confidentiality while the experiments were being conducted."

Doc narrowed his eyes. "Technically speaking, bringing black market equipment on board a spaceship is against federation rules. You could be brought up on charges."

"I know. And I wasn't planning on applying for a position on Moon Trek 6, but when I found out Captain Ryder was in charge, I—" I looked down at my hands in my lap. "I changed my mind. There aren't a lot of Plunians left in the galaxy, and I would have regretted the decision not to be a part of her crew."

"I see," Doc said. His tone of voice had softened, just like I'd predicted. "What happens to the experiment now?"

"Not a whole lot. The range of the comm is short-lived. Technically, I fulfilled my part of the agreement before Moon Unit 6 departed. Payment was transferred to an account in my name, and the device was shut off. There's been no risk to Moon Unit 6 while I've been on board."

Doc said nothing. The next few seconds were crucial. Yes, he was a doctor first and a senior officer second, but he'd also been trained to spot lies, and he had the power to have me thrown in lock-up if he questioned my loyalties. Basic federation training required him to be able to assess a threat. So I stared at the spot on the bridge of Doc's nose and thought about comforting things like playing catch with my dad before he sold out our family for thirty pieces of silver.

Tiny thoughts tickled my brain. What time was it? Did Neptune know where I was? What else had Daila told Doc—and had she made a report to anyone else?

I mentally wrestled the thoughts aside. Bridge of Doc's nose. Bridge of Doc's nose. Bridge of Doc's nose.

"...are you listening to me?" Doc asked.

"What?" I followed the question up with a head tilt and a few soft whacks to my ear to make it look like I was having difficulty hearing and not preoccupied with a secret mission to distract the second in command while sneaking someone onto the ship.

Fortunately, the recently removed comm device and vertigo were a good enough cover story for Doc to buy my act. He scanned me with a wand and recorded the readings. "You're still on the cold side." He handed me a thermal blanket. "Lay down, Lieutenant. Rest. I'll be back to check on you later." He yawned.

"What time is it?"

"Zulu Three point five. Get some sleep. That's what the rest of the ship is doing." He glanced at the body on the cart next to me. "Sorry about that. I'll have my team move her out of your way." He patted me on the shoulder and left.

One crisis averted, another one presented. I felt like I was running the gauntlet in a forbidden zone. One false step and this whole thing would blow up in my face.

Two medics entered. They were dressed in blue uniforms, which indicated their position in Medi-Bay. Unlike Doc, their sleeves were black. These were the uniforms worn by the team that dealt with body disposal.

Yuck.

I pulled the thermal blanket closer to ward off the chill that thought brought on. The taller of the two medics, a fit bald man with elaborate tattoos decorating his scalp, strode to the far end of Xina's cart. "We ran out of room, and the living passengers took priority. Doc didn't want to put her into the vault until he had a chance to run her diagnostic panel, but now that you're here, he changed his mind."

"You'll want to hold onto that blanket," the other man said. This one was built like an apple, the fabric of his uniform stretched across his midsection. Unlike Ofra, he'd accepted the standard issue uniform even though it barely fit. "The vault is refrigerated, and you'll feel the chill as soon as we open the door."

I kept the blanket around me and watched the two men roll Xina's cart to a wall filled with small, metal doors. The tattooed man opened a door at waist height and pulled out a slab. They lifted Xina, moved her onto the slab, and slid the slab back into the wall. He was right about the temperature. Crisp tendrils of dry air wrapped their fingers around my skin despite the blanket, and the memory of the bone-chilling cold I'd felt after Daila injected me in the uniform ward came flooding back. I fought the paralytic sensation. When the medics were done, they pushed the cart back into place next to me.

"There," said the pudgy man. "It's like she wasn't even here."

The tattooed man smiled. "Luxury accommodations, right? Just be glad you're not in there with the Martians."

The medics left. They were right; I was glad not to be in the other room with the Martians, but not for the reason they suspected.

For starters, I'd just determined a way to get out of Medi-Morgue, and I doubted the Martians would have stood by and watched while I stole a body and staged it to look like me.

30: RISK ASSESSMENT: OFF THE CHARTS

It took less time to remove Xina's body from the refrigerated unit than I'd expected. Despite her height, she was painfully thin, which made her easy to maneuver. I placed her body on my cart, stripped off Ofra's uniform top and pulled it onto Xina's frail body. This was definitely a job for my unemotional Plunian side because if my earthling half stopped to think about what I was doing, I'd be seriously creeped out.

When Xina was as dressed as I could get her, I laid her onto her side and covered her with the thermal blanket. I left my helmet sitting on the cart by her head for no reason other than if Doc sent someone in to see how I was doing, they'd be suspicious if the helmet was gone. Before I snuck out, I jimmied the lock on the medicine cabinet and stole two oxygen tablets as a precautionary measure.

From what I'd learned of the ship schematics, there was only one way out of Medi-Bay, and that was through the doors from which I'd entered. What wasn't public knowledge was that Medi-Morgue had a separate entrance and exit for one very practical reason: if a corpse was considered dangerous in any way, there needed to be a way to transport it without contamination. The seams to that door were almost undetectable, but after running my fingertips over the wall, I found them. I stepped on a button on the floor that activated the doors and, as soon as they opened, departed. With any luck, I'd be back under the thermal blanket before anybody noticed I was gone. But considering the past several hours, the last thing I was counting on was luck.

Assuming I'd lost twenty minutes making Xina's corpse pass for me (yuck!), I didn't have a lot of time to get to the rocket nozzle. Which meant HVPTS. I found the nearest one, slapped the launch button, and zapped through the ship in seconds. I tumbled out and bumped into a pair of legs.

I looked up. Anatol.

"Lieutenant Stryker. I was starting to think you had second thoughts."

"There's not much that could have kept me away," I said honestly.

He nodded slightly in response.

This was my first time seeing the rocket nozzle up close. The beryllium spheres sat in a contained chamber in the middle of the room. The floor was rigid, painted with magnetic paint. My boots felt heavy as I crossed the room. "The engines are off?" I asked.

"They are slowing. They will officially shut down in two minutes."

"Have you seen the drones yet?"

"No."

The chief science officer answered each of my questions. So much was riding on the next half hour and Neptune and my ability to trick Anatol and get Zeke on board. I didn't know where Neptune was or if he even knew I was there. For all I knew, he thought I'd failed or reneged on my promise to help.

I put my hands on the white railing that ran the perimeter of the room and stared out the windows. Even with no mission, I could look out these windows for hours. Precious few got to see what I was looking at. Vantablack skies. Twinkling stars and planets. Shimmery trails from comets and asteroids, particles left behind by matter floating with no destination. Faint outlines of planets that were lightyears beyond our location. Someday I hoped to say I'd seen them all.

I recognized the outline of Venus, closer than the other planets since it was Moon Unit 6's destination. From there it was easy to look to the left, approximately fifty-three million miles west of Venus, and imagine where Plunia had been. Even if it weren't too far to see with the naked eye, there'd be nothing there.

But tonight, there was. A fleet of white drones closed in on the ship. I watched, mesmerized, as the round white discs approached in a neat formation and then spread out at equal intervals within inches of the exterior. The top and bottom of each drone widened, like the bun on an yttrium burger putting distance between itself and the patty within, and sharp tool-like tentacles extended.

"I find it relaxing to watch drones repair a ship in motion," Anatol said.

"How do they know where to begin? You sent the report to request them, but they seem to be hovering. Almost like they're trying to determine where to start."

"They are. The drones are programmed to find the center of the threat and repair from there. Right now, they're assessing the condition of the spheres."

The drones weren't repairing the ship because they didn't know where to start. And unless Anatol looked away long enough for me to toss a lighter into the chamber with the spheres, we were S.O.L.

The activity of the drones was mesmerizing, but the fear of being found out left me cold. The mission had failed. Anatol wasn't going to take my word for it that the drones were necessary, and he wasn't going to leave the rocket nozzle and trust my report that they'd done their job. If Zeke was in his repair pod outside the ship, he had seconds to get through the hatch. Seconds that were ticking away, and with them any hope Neptune had of covering up what he'd done and getting to Venus to rescue his sister. I stared out into the darkness and I knew if there was a chance I could help him, I would. Even with everything I knew—or didn't know—about him, I'd be on his side.

The realization lit a fire within me, and created the first true flicker of warmth since Daila shot me with the Anti-Vert. I looked down at my hands. My coloring was returning, from sterling to lavender. And I became aware that I was no longer alone by the windows. I felt, rather than saw, Neptune. I turned, and we locked eyes.

"Stryker," Neptune said. The look on his face was unreadable, but the tension coming off him wasn't. He put his hands on the rail. I turned back to the windows and put my hands on the rail next to his.

"It's hard to imagine how much life is out there," he said quietly. "Survivors fighting for a future. Wrongly accused who get up every day and hope to get free. Victims who don't accept their circumstances."

"Some of the accused are guilty and deserve to be locked up," I said.

Neptune shifted his hand, and pressed it against mine. A flush came over me and my coloring grew brighter. Neptune had no idea how welcome the warmth was. He only knew it would create the diversion we needed to fool Anatol.

The drones broke formation and suctioned onto the ship. Drones in the rear buzzed in circles, flashing red lights that indicated they were functioning in emergency repair mode. It worked!

I watched while the drones completed their task. Filled with euphoria, I looked at Neptune, expecting a crack in his exterior—something to indicate that he felt what I felt.

He bent his head down, his lips next to my ear. Sharing a confidence in front of Anatol was risky, and Neptune had to know that. Whatever was on his mind must have been important. He was risking his mission to make sure I heard.

"Your father isn't guilty," he said.

31: THINK YOU KNOW THE TRUTH?

NEPTUNE'S EYES WERE DARK, A SHADE CLOSER to the skies outside the ship than anything I'd seen. The heat within me turned off like a switch had been thrown, and I stepped away from him. He was using me. Using my dad. Using what my dad had done to manipulate me.

"No," I said. He reached out for my wrist, and I yanked my arm away from him. I took two more steps backward, facing him, and then turned toward Anatol. "I trust you received a report from Captain Ryder on my incident in the uniform ward earlier tonight?"

"Yes," Anatol said. "I admit I did not expect to see you here tonight."

"It was important to me to prove my interest in the ship to you."

"And you have, Lieutenant. I will include that in my report."

"Permission to return to Medi-Bay," I said.

"Permission granted."

I left the rocket nozzle without looking back. For the first time since boarding Moon Unit 6, the seven seconds on the HVPTS felt like a lifetime.

I didn't go straight to Medi-Morgue. The Martians were out of commission in Medi-Bay, Neptune was with Anatol, and Pika was in my room. All of which was fine by me. I'd taken a ton of risks to help Neptune, and he betrayed me. He used the one thing I wanted to believe, the thing I wouldn't allow myself to consider because the damaging reality would destroy me, and he used it against me to further his needs. I hated him. I didn't care if he succeeded in finding Vesta. Neptune claimed my reality had inspired him to save her. That was probably part of the manipulation too.

It no longer mattered how much I'd wanted to be a member of security. I could be cold and removed from reality, but deep down, I knew if it came to me using the secrets—the weaknesses—I learned about someone to gain an edge over them, I wouldn't want to do it. There had to be some humanity in the galaxy, and even if I was only half human, I was going to respect that half to uphold the memory of my mother.

I went to the bridge. There was one person on

this ship who I felt would understand my anger and my sense of loss and it was Captain Ryder. It would be some time before Doc discovered that I'd snuck out of Medi-Morgue, or for Daila to submit a report about our incident in the uniform ward. For all I knew, Ofra would report me for not delivering his uniform as promised.

It didn't matter. None of it mattered. All I needed was a chance to unburden myself with my side of the story and explain why I'd lied about the need for a drone army to create a diversion. It was a gamble on my part, but with nothing else to believe in, I was desperate to believe that the only other Plunian on board Moon Unit 6 would understand. Neptune was caught up in a mission that benefitted himself, and by using the ship to achieve his agenda, he was risking too much. The needs of the many outweighed the needs of the one. Neptune was but one, and it was up to me to expose his risks.

The bridge was quiet. I'd forgotten that we had scheduled our faked crisis for the portion of the trek when the ship was on autopilot. My arrival was ignored by the skeleton crew working the overnight shift and acknowledged by the personnel director, TJ Woodward, who appeared to be observing. His glossy black hair was styled as usual, side part and slicked back away from his face. The hollows under his eyes indicated he wasn't used to keeping round-the-clock hours.

He stood and addressed me officially. "Lieutenant Stryker," he said. "I'm conducting performance reviews. What brings you to the bridge? Is there a problem with your new assignment?" He looked almost hopeful. Was it too much to ask that someone other than the person manipulating me believed I could do my job?

"I'm adjusting to my new assignment as best as I can," I said honestly. "I was hoping to find Captain Ryder for private counsel."

"The captain is in her quarters. She's expected to return to the bridge at Zulu Seven."

"What time is it now?"

"Just after Zulu Five."

"Thank you." I turned to leave.

"Lieutenant Stryker," the personnel director called. I turned back. He held up his index finger and appeared to be listening to a private transmission. "Captain Ryder requests you join her in her quarters in Sector 1."

"Now?"

He smiled, caught off guard by my lack of formality. "Yes." He paused for a moment, then added, "she's looking forward to it."

That was the first comforting thing I'd heard all day. I left the bridge and walked the quiet corridors to Sector 1. Top ranking officers were assigned quarters close to the bridge, not because Moon Unit Corporation was concerned about threats to the ship, but because it looked good. Aside from myself, I had no idea how the crew was compensated, but it stood to reason that the appearance of luxury quarters for those in charge would mean something to the passengers.

Captain Ryder's door opened to me before I had a chance to knock. She welcomed me with a much-needed hug and ushered me inside. "Sylvia," she said, "you have no idea how happy I am that you're safe."

"Captain, I need to make a report about a crew member. I'll leave it up to you to decide what to do."

The captain pressed a series of buttons on an unmarked keypad next to the door, and a red light glowed overhead. She had activated the sound barrier. Whatever we said while inside her room would remain confidential. She was giving me an opportunity to talk freely without fear of retribution.

"As you know, I've been reassigned from uniform management to security section."

"Yes," she said. "Neptune told me that's where you should have been stationed from the start."

"You talked to Neptune about me?"

"He is one of the most respected men in the universe. Not to mention feared."

"Doesn't that bother you? You're piloting a spaceship with him as your protection. What if he went rogue? Used the ship for his own purposes? What if he manipulated crew members into positions that could gain access to restricted parts of the vessel to sneak additional people on board? Right under the noses of the very people who have the most reason not to trust him?"

Captain Ryder studied me. The severity of my accusations hung in the air, spoken as a hypothetical, but detailed enough to let her speculate on their possible truth. In fact, that's what she was doing. Running my statement through her mental screener, determining whether I was speaking emotionally as a part human or objectively as a part Plunian. I sat up straighter and looked her in the eye. I wanted her to know this wasn't a case of hurt feelings or broken heart. These were honest-to-goodness concerns about Moon Unit 6 and the happenings on board it.

"Sylvia, any member of Moon Unit 5 was automatically approved for work aboard Moon Unit 6."

"I heard that, but the circumstances surrounding my employment on Moon Unit 5 were..." I didn't finish that thought. "I didn't know if the same standards would apply to me as the others."

"You are qualified to work for this company. Your loss was my loss. I appreciate the respect you show by confiding in me, and using the discretion allowed me in my role as captain, I'd like to return the favor."

Here it comes, I thought. The captain had all but told me she trusted Neptune implicitly. I braced myself. I was about to get a one-way pass back to the space station, credentials stripped for good this time, and a black mark on my record for reporting my superior. Worse, Neptune would find out and know I undermined his mission.

My life dream, gone. I'd trained for it, studied for it, and when I was forced to drop out of Space Academy, continued learning on my own. Everything I'd added to my skill set had led me to this moment, and I'd failed.

"Go ahead, Captain. I'm prepared to accept your response and decision regarding my future."

"Your future is to remain in your role and assist Neptune in his mission to find and rescue his sister."

Shock at learning Katherine already knew about Neptune's agenda left me feeling duped. All the knowledge I'd considered to be sacrosanct had been common. "You know what he's trying to do?" I asked.

"Lieutenant, I've known about Neptune's mission from the start. I wanted to tell you that I knew but he cautioned me about trading on our friendship. His assessment was that you would perform better if you felt you were operating on a team of two."

"No," I said. "He used me. He used us both. Just now, at the rocket nozzle, he told me my father—"

"He told you your father isn't guilty." Captain Ryder smiled tenderly.

"Yes. Why would he say something like that?"

"Because it's the truth."

32: YOU DON'T KNOW JACK

"Jack Stryker was tried for suspicion of collusion with space pirates," I said. For the first time since it had happened, I found myself arguing the one thing I never wanted to believe. "He was judged by Federation Council and found guilty by a vote of twenty-two to one abstain. He's serving a life sentence for trading on his loyalties to his family and planet for financial gain."

Captain Ryder's eyes flicked up to the red light glowing over our head. "That is the story Federation Council wants you to believe."

"Federation Council approved a relief fund for Plunians but nobody told me. Why? Why would Neptune keep that from me?"

"You are asking very good questions. To say more would put many people in danger. You need to find out for yourself, Sylvia. Assemble your own team. Design a mission to learn the truth. Only then will you understand what kind of work you've trained to do."

She stood up and deactivated the sound barrier. The red light went out. "Lieutenant Stryker, Moon Unit 6 is simply a cruise ship that offers travel to unique destinations in the galaxy. Our paid passengers expect a pleasant, relaxing trip that offers a few luxuries they might not experience in their regular lives. That being said, I appreciate the commitment you bring to your position, and I thank you for your service. I'll notify your direct supervisor of your actions and request he reward you accordingly."

Translation: she was going to tell Neptune I came to her and advise him to view the act as me being a good security agent. "Thank you, Captain."

"Lieutenant," she said. "You will be relieved of duties for the duration of today. Please return to Medi-Bay immediately and remain there until Doc deems your physical readings are back to acceptable levels."

"Yes, Captain."

I left her quarters. Soon, the ship would be buzzing with passengers lining up in the observation deck, getting breakfast in the Space Bar, or checking in on today's entertainment. Crew members would report for duty at their assigned posts. And, assuming the effects of tainted protein packs would metabolize like any other food source, the Martians would be released from Medi-Bay.

And once Medi-Bay was clear, Doc would discover the corpse in Medi-Morgue that was dressed up to pass for me.

Neptune's problems were going to have to get in line.

I arrived at Medi-Morgue and slipped into the secret entry. The cart with Xina's body was where I left it, her body still resting on the side, and my helmet on the table next to her. If anyone had gotten close and checked on her/me, they would have immediately known what I had done. But if that were the case, I doubted they'd leave her where she was. I was hopeful that any checks on my condition had been of the peeking-through-the-door variety.

I crept toward the cart, bracing myself for a possibly worse Yuck! moment than before since I had no idea what changes an unrefrigerated fake-Venusian corpse might have gone through in the time I'd left her lying under the thermal blanket. I picked up my helmet and set it on the floor and then slowly pulled the blanket away from the body.

And stifled a scream. Because the corpse wasn't a corpse. The body was very much alive.

33: SUCCESS?

SILVER SPARKLES FLUTTERED THROUGH THE AIR as the body under the blanket sat up and swung at me. I reacted on instinct and blocked her punch. The figure rose from the cart and spun toward me, creating a distracting tornado of glitter. I anticipated the move and leaned back, avoiding contact. When I straightened, I used a sweeping kick to knock her legs out from under her. She jumped with knees bent, high enough to avoid the strike, and landed butt-first on the cart.

Only one person had ever jumped high enough to clear my sweeping kick. Zeke Champion.

Stunned, I stopped fighting and looked at the Venusian's face. It was Zeke, covered in sparkly powder and dressed in Ofra Starr's baggy uniform. "Sylvia! Long time no see!" He hopped down from the cart and hugged me.

Aside from the sparkles, Zeke looked like he always looked. Sturdy build and freckles from working in the sun dotted his face under the powder. His broad smile showed where he'd lost a tooth during an early attempt to rewire a drone. The gap should have made him appear creepy, but instead, it just made him look young.

I pushed him away and hissed, "What are you doing here?"

"Did you forget the mission?"

"No, I didn't forget the mission. I mean *here*. In Medi-Morgue. Aren't you supposed to be hacking into the flight memory and erasing the need for the drones? Or overriding Xina's medical history before Anatol accesses it and finds out the truth?"

"Done and done. I'm very efficient." He hung his head down and ran his fingers over his floppy hair. "But I am never going to get rid of this glitter."

There were too many questions to ask and not enough time for answers. I grabbed the hem of the shirt on Zeke, yanked it over his head. The uniform, while ill-fitting on someone of Zeke's frame, at least made him look like a member of Moon Unit crew. Without Ofra's shirt, the outfit Zeke had traveled in was exposed: dirt colored trousers, dirt colored long sleeved shirt, dirt covered tunic. The shade helped him blend in on his home planet. On a newly designed luxury cruise ship, not so much. I shoved Ofra's shirt back at him. "Put that back on."

I climbed onto the cart and lay down where Zeke had been, pulling the thermal blanket up over me. "You have to get out of here before anybody finds you."

"And go where? My repair pod is tethered to the valve cover outside the hatch. The drones are flying in formation behind it. If my dad finds out I took a whole fleet of them, he'll send me to Colony 10 to work on their sanitation system."

"What did Neptune tell you to do?"

"He said to wait in Medi-Morgue until you showed up and you'd tell me what to do. When I got here and found that thing on a cart with your helmet, I figured you wanted it to look like it was you. But to be honest, it didn't smell so good, so I had to get rid of it."

I shuddered at Zeke's disassociated reference to Xina's corpse. Maybe he referred to her as "it" because that was the only way he could deal. The impersonal nature of it was off-putting.

I cut my eyes from Zeke to the refrigeration units and back to Zeke. "What did you do with—what was there?"

"I put it in the chute."

"What chute?"

"I don't know. That chute." He pointed to a

circular door on the wall. My heart sank. "What is that, the trash chute?"

"No, Zeke, that's not the trash chute. That's the laundry chute."

"You're kidding."

I only wish I were. Because Zeke had accidentally transferred Xina's body back to where it had been when I found it.

"You have to get to the uniform ward, like, immediately."

"Okay, let's go."

"I can't leave. Any minute now, Doc is going to come through that door to check on me."

"Considering Anatol knows you weren't in Medi-Bay when you and Neptune did your little heat trick at the rocket nozzle, isn't it going to seem a little more suspicious if you're here?"

Zeke was right. Which meant we both had to get to the uniform ward and, avoiding the passenger corridors and the HVPTS, there was only one way to get there fast.

Yuck.

34: DUMMY LUCK

I shoved Zeke into the chute first. The look he gave me was not particularly appreciative. I grabbed my helmet and dove in after him, swinging the door shut behind me. We landed in a heap: me on top of Zeke on top of Xina's body. A cloud of sparkles puffed out of the laundry cart over our heads.

Zeke scrambled to get out. "That was fun," he said. He brushed the glitter off one sleeve and then the other.

I climbed out. "What is wrong with you?"

"Me? I'm not the one who forgot how to say thank you. What happened, Syl, did you lose your sense of fun and adventure when you took this job?"

I stared at him. "Me? I'm exactly how I should be. Creeped out by what we just did."

"I don't know what you're talking about. That was a rush, and the glitter made it even better."

"Zeke, you just dumped a corpse down a laundry chute and then jumped in and landed on top of her. And then you called it fun. I don't care how many good times we had these last few months. Right now, I feel like I don't even know you."

Zeke's face paled. "What are you talking about? A corpse. Right." He held his hands up. "Like I'm going to touch a corpse." He pointed over my shoulder. "That's a sack of glitter with some bones in it."

Hearing him talk about the murdered Venusian turned my stomach, but there wasn't time to school him on life and death and the implied respect one earned by passing between those two states of being. I turned back to the laundry cart and grabbed Xina. A cloud of glitter released through stretched Stealthyester®. The seam on the fabric frayed open and a stream of glitter and sand fell out. "What the heck?" I said.

Zeke joined me. "It's a dummy," he said. "Filled with cosmic dust. Someone tore it open and added glitter and did a poor job sewing the seam." He bent down and grabbed the lumpy figure, and together we pulled it out of the cart and onto the floor of the uniform ward. I stood by the feet, and Zeke stood by the head. The face was blank with Xs marking the eyes, nose, mouth, and ears.

It was a standard issue medical dummy. We trained with them at Space Academy to get experience with an injured or unconscious member of the team. There was no leaving behind an injured party. We deployed as a unit and we returned as a unit. All for one and one for all.

Neptune had been counting on that. When he confided in me that he needed my help, it was because he knew I wouldn't abandon him, and I'd done just that. I left him to fight for his sister on his own, and I'd gone straight to the captain to turn him in. It was only when she soundproofed the room and told me that she was aware of what he was doing that I recognized everything he'd done had been for one purpose: to keep me focused. I'd been so cold when I arrived at the rocket nozzle thanks to the injected Anti-Vert, but Neptune's close contact had generated the heat we needed.

My only concern had been how to generate enough heat to fake Anatol into believing the repair drones were necessary. But once the drones were in place, we needed them to get an accurate reading on the condition of Moon Unit 6, and that meant the heat had to cease. Fast. And Neptune knew he had to interrupt whatever Venus-adjacent current ran between us. He broke a top-level classified chain of intel to shock me with the truth about my dad to do so.

And it had worked. I'd gotten mad, I'd pulled

away from him, and the electric current that faked out the drone sensors was interrupted as easily as a plug being pulled out of a socket.

We were in it together.

"Zeke, how did you know to look for me in Medi-Morgue?"

"I heard you on your comm device, at least until it went out. You screamed. And then I heard someone else saying you needed medical attention. She had a nice voice. Who was that?"

"Forget her. You could hear me?"

"Yes. Why?"

"Yeoman Teron shot me with an Anti-Vert pellet, and it fried the comm. I went deaf in that ear. My equilibrium was off, and I blacked out. When I woke up, I was in Medi-Morgue next to Xina Astryd's body."

Zeke didn't say anything, so I continued. "When Doc came to check on me, he asked about the comm. I told him it was a paid experiment testing next-gen equipment and there wasn't time to have it removed before Moon Unit 6 departed. He seemed to buy that."

Zeke cut his eyes from me to the medical dummy. Between words like "Morgue" and "Xina Astryd's body," I knew he was putting two and two together, but I rushed ahead while I still had at least a fraction of his attention. "The Martians took up all the room in Medi-Bay—the tainted protein packs—so the only place for me to sleep off the aftereffects was in the morgue. Doc put Xina's body in a refrigeration unit, but I had to get to the rocket nozzle to help Neptune, so we could get you onto the ship. I pulled her body out and left her on the cart. To anybody who didn't look closely, they'd think it was me."

This time Zeke's attention was 100 percent on the medical dummy. "You thought I threw a corpse in the laundry chute," he said. "You thought I jumped into the laundry chute and landed on her and said it was fun."

"I told you you were acting weird," I said. "The Zeke I know passed out in biology when we dissected a toad."

I looked up just in time to see Zeke's eyeballs roll to the back of his head and his body collapse on the floor on top of a fresh pile of glitter. At least when I passed out, there was a legitimate medical explanation.

This was not the time to judge or feel superior. This was the time to assess the mounting list of problems facing me. Zeke's body on the floor wasn't nearly as much of a problem now as it would be if someone discovered him on board the ship. Problem number one was to hide him.

Now that I knew a Venusian body hadn't

recently been in the laundry cart, it seemed as good a place as any. I hoisted Zeke over my shoulder and tossed him in on a pile of uniforms. I grabbed additional garments from the closet that Daila had used to keep me warm earlier that evening and threw them on top of him.

The more pressing issue was to assess everything I knew based on the medical dummy.

Someone knew Xina's body had been on the medical cart. Someone knew she'd been dressed in Ofra's uniform next to my helmet. It stood to reason that someone knew I'd been the one to put her there.

Assessment #1: I was visible.

Whoever had been in Medi-Morgue had moved Xina's body. Where? Was it back in the refrigeration unit or elsewhere? Her body would allow someone to run a medical panel or examine her closely enough to determine she was chipped. And not Venusian.

Assessment #2: The junk DNA profile Zeke had uploaded was at risk of being exposed.

Assessment #3: Exposure of tampering with passenger medical files would start an investigation that would lead directly to Neptune. Or me.

Neptune was a highly decorated ex-military man with a mostly spotless record. I had a history that as recently as the last Moon Unit included hacking into the database and uploading my identification on top of another person's medical profile. If push came to shove, the accusatory finger would point at me.

I could take the fall for this. It was my turn to pay Neptune back for trusting me with his mission.

35: SLAP HAPPY

I HAD TO THINK. AND FOR THE FIRST TIME since Moon Unit 6 had departed, I had complete silence in which to do so. It was the most distracting silence I'd ever experienced.

I sat on the bench on the far end of the uniform ward. Neptune's mission was simple: rescue his sister. He had agreed to help an escaped convict reach a doctor who could remove her tracking chip in exchange for information that would lead him to his sibling.

But the escaped convict was dead.

Who had killed her? And why?

The suspect list depended on who knew what.

It struck me as sad that up to now, nobody had been asking who killed Xina. The attention surrounding her had been about covering up who she was. First, with potions and powders to enhance the appearance of her being a Venusian. And in Medi-Morgue, dressing her up like me. Now her body had been stolen. What if we were wrong to focus on the mission? What if the mission —the desire to get to Venus to rescue Vesta at all costs—had nothing to do with Xina's murder? What if she'd been killed for a completely unrelated reason, and our interference put everyone at risk?

Two possible answers: Vesta would never get rescued, or the promise of Vesta's presence on Venus was a trap. Either way, Neptune needed to know more than he did, starting with the truth about Xina.

I ran back to the laundry cart and lifted Zeke by his shirt. "Champion! Wake up!" When his eyes didn't open, I slapped him across the face. His eyes fluttered and closed and then popped open.

"Tell me what you know about Xina Astryd. The criminal record, the reason she was chipped, the medical files, everything you found out when you first accessed her data."

"It's gone. Her data was wiped when I uploaded the junk DNA."

"I'm sorry," I said.

"For what?"

I slapped him again.

He stared straight ahead and spoke. "Xina Astryd. Daughter of Venusian and Saturnian Pilot. Part of a Federation Council experiment to develop a race of cross-breed alien women to use in secret intelligence missions. Chipped at birth. Arrested for killing a security agent at the Intergalactic Supernova Museum during the theft of the Federation Council's collection of black carbonado diamonds. Spent seven years in solitary confinement and was moved to Colony 13 to serve out the remainder of her sentence. She fit a profile that matched Neptune's inquiries about his sister and was released to engage him in a rescue mission."

Zeke recited the words as if they'd been programmed into a folder inside his brain, unregistered as anything of value, merely a byproduct of having seen the information while in the network. It happened with people who worked in intelligence. They were exposed to vast amounts of data in the course of their deployments, and since their conscious brain was focused on the mission, the extemporaneous details of what they saw and heard often were lost before anyone knew they'd been registered at all. Had Zeke not passed out at the suggestion that he'd manhandled a corpse and enjoyed his subsequent tangle with it in the laundry cart, I possibly would have lost my window to retrieve his temporary memories. It was a small win in my favor.

The win was less impactful considering I didn't know who else on the ship was interested in the information about Xina. And knowing Neptune might be too close to the situation to ask him these questions, I recognized my role on the team. I had questions too, questions about him and what he knew about my dad, but now wasn't the time to put my agenda before his. Besides, I'd accessed the files about Neptune in Lumiere's database and had sent them to Cat. I could comb through them as much as I wanted when this was over.

Holy moon rocks. How had I forgotten about the files I'd copied from Independent Border Patrol? Not only had I gotten Neptune's, but I'd gotten Xina's too. And assuming Pika hadn't broken Cat as she had in the past, the files were stored in a pattern of digital bytes inside the feline robot's head.

I ran from the uniform ward to my quarters to find Pika on the table looking up. "I didn't do it," she said.

I followed her stare to a small nook where the wall and the ceiling seam met. Wedged in the space was Cat, upside down, feet sticking out, eyes blinking an error message in code.

"You're not in trouble," I said. Under any other circumstances, she was, but if she felt threatened, she'd shrink, and I needed her to be at her full size. "I have to talk to Cat." I looked around the room for something to stand on.

I didn't need to stand on anything. I could turn off the gravity.

I hit the switch and yanked my boots off in a pile. Slowly, I floated up, into mid-air. "Give me a push," I said.

"I can't," Pika said. I looked down for her and saw her floating next to me. I reached out to leverage myself against her, but she was so light I succeeded only in pushing her toward the bed. Her face scrunched into a pout, and she crossed her arms. Seconds later, she floated back up to where I was. Both of us were still out of reach of Cat's position on the wall.

I scissor-kicked my feet and waved my arms to try to rise, but nothing worked. I would have been better off stacking the furniture by the wall and scaling it or having Pika climb onto my shoulders.

We could still do that.

I grabbed Pika's wrist. She tried to pull away, but I kept hold. "You're not in trouble," I said again. "But it's important that I talk to Cat. Climb up me and see if you can reach him."

"Okay, okay, okay," she said. She slowly scaled my torso, grabbing fistfuls of uniform. The faster she tried to go, the less successful our attempts. In time, she stood with both feet on my head and stretched. I couldn't watch because moving my head would have upset her balance, so I stared at a spot on the wall and hoped for the best.

But sadly, it wasn't my day. Because before Pika could knock Cat loose, the doors to my quarters swished open, and a deep, scary voice surprised us both.

"What are you doing?" Neptune asked.

Pika toppled off my head and floated in a backward flip through the room. It was as graceful a maneuver as any I'd seen, and I would have tried it myself if Neptune hadn't clamped onto my ankle and yanked me down to the ground.

36: RAG TAG CREW

"Ow!" I yelled. "Watch it."

"What are you trying to do?" Neptune demanded, switching the gravity back on.

"I need Cat. He's holding important data that we need to see before we make our next move."

The expression on Neptune's face temporarily fell into confusion. At that moment I knew the answers to several of the questions that had been stacking up in my brain. Neptune had no idea what the past several hours had been like for me.

I held my hand palm-side out. "Let me make a report."

"Go."

"I stole some files from the border patrol database. I buried them in the uniform ward master computer under Care Instructions for

Stealthyester®, but when I went to retrieve them, I found Pika and Ofra Starr in the hallway."

"The engineer?"

"Yes. The man wears custom uniforms, and both got dirty. He needed to pick up the one he sent to us earlier, but the new uniform lieutenant"—I tipped my head in Pika's direction—"didn't have a chance to get it clean."

"That's an incomplete report."

"Let me finish. I sent Pika and Ofra away and got into the uniform ward, but Daila was there. That woman has it in for me. Is that your fault?"

Oops, we were back to the intimidating scowl. "I accessed the computer and sent the files to Cat's data chip," I pointed to the robot cat wedged into the ceiling seam, "and then Daila shot me with Anti-Vert and I got really, really cold and ended up in Medi-Morgue where Doc submerged me in Goop to revive me." I paused for a moment. "That's a technical term," I added.

"You made it to the rocket nozzle anyway."

"That was the mission."

We didn't have time for the moments of unspoken conversation that passed between us. Or maybe we did. We each had different pieces of the same puzzle, and the clock was ticking on our time to put it together.

"How did you get into the IBP database?"

"I used Lumiere's computer."

"When?"

"After dinner last night. The proximity to Venus got him all charged up. I used the opportunity to get into his room. I pretended—never mind what I pretended. I made him a drink, he fell asleep, and I logged into his computer."

"What kind of drink?"

"A Methanol Intoxicant Cocktail."

"You slipped him a Mickey?"

"Oh sure, you're okay with 'Mickey' but not 'Goop'?"

Neptune crossed his arms. "What will happen when Lumiere wakes up and discovers you're not there?"

"I don't know. Maybe he'll assume I got bored and left and he'll go to bed. I mean, it'll be a little embarrassing the next time I see him, but nothing we both can't handle. We're adults, right? Sometimes things just don't work out."

Neptune turned around, and I grabbed his arm. My fingers slipped off his giant bicep, and I tried to grab him again. This time it was more like a swat. He grabbed my wrist and held tight. My skin turned bright purple.

"I don't have time to discuss your love life," he said.

And I had no time to waste lying about why I wanted Lumiere's files in the first place. "What if Xina's murder had nothing to do with Vesta?" I said. "I get that you're focused on saving your sister's life and Xina was your ticket, but Xina was a criminal. It's possible somebody else wanted her dead. It's possible IBP was tracking her all along. We need to see her criminal record. *That's* why I hacked into Lumiere's database."

"Mr. Neptune?" Pika said in a very soft voice. I'd forgotten all about her, and when I turned my head, I realized why. She'd shrunken in on herself. She sat on top of the table with her legs bent and her arms wrapped around them, making her look almost as much like a toy as Cat. "Don't yell at Sylvia," she said.

"Stay out of this, Pika," he growled.

"No," she said. She unfolded her arms and legs and stood up. She was shaking with nerves, but she didn't back down from Neptune like so many others did. "Sylvia is my friend. She covered for me when I didn't clean my new friend's uniform, and she lets me stay here because she knows I'm afraid of the green meanies."

I watched Pika stand up for herself and me, to a man who intimidated half of the universe. A thin, pink Gremlon was willing to defend me to him. It was the second time since my dad brought shame to our family that I recognized the influence I'd had on someone else.

I put my hand out and Pika took it. I turned to Neptune. "You want to find your sister. That is your mission, but you can't do it alone. You can have a team if you want but you have to trust us."

"What does Pika bring to the team?"

"I can make things sparkly," she said.

Neptune glanced up at the seam and then back to me. He then looked back and forth between Pika and my faces. "Pika, get Cat."

"Pika can't get Cat," I said.

"Yes, I can," Pika said. She faced the wall and looked up. Her slightly webbed hands laid flat against the surface, and she scaled it. There were many things I didn't know about Gremlons, among them the fact that they had small suction cups embedded in their palms. It was a handy time to discover it.

"You knew she could do that?" I asked Neptune.

"You didn't?"

Pika reached the ceiling and grabbed Cat. The robotic pet let out a loud meow. "Now you be quiet," Pika said to it. The meow transitioned to a purr. "That's better." Pika tucked Cat under her chin and came back down. Under any other circumstances, I would have laughed at how she looked like a mama cat herself, but this wasn't the time for jokes or ribbing. It was time to find out who we were dealing with and what we could do about it.

When I first customized Cat, I rewired him and

added several circuit boards that stored data, created sounds, reacted to audible and visual stimuli, and made him move and sound like a cat. It was this last aspect that had enamored Pika of the toy. Colony 7, where she lived, was filled with feral felines, and even though Cat was made from plastic, Pika treated him like a pet of her own.

I tipped Cat face-down on the table and used a small toolkit to open his rear panel. Pika grabbed him off the table and held him out of reach. "Don't you hurt him!" she said.

We'd created a monster. "He's not hurt. Watch." I addressed the toy. "Cat, are you hurt?"

"Meow."

"Do you want to help Neptune?"

"Meow."

"Is Pika your friend?"

"Meow."

"Enough," Neptune said.

"Meow."

Pika handed Cat back to me. I cradled him in the crook of my arm while his activated sound chip purred on a loop.

"Don't you think you should be getting to the uniform ward?" I asked. "That's your job, remember?"

"You did my job yesterday," she said. "There's nothing left to do."

"That's not true. Your new friend Ofra needs

his uniform. And there's someone in the laundry cart who needs to be outfitted. Can you help them?"

"Can Cat help me?" she asked.

"No, I'm afraid he can't. Cat has a job to do too. We all have jobs to make the mission successful. Maybe if you show Cat you can do your job, it'll be easier for him to do his?"

"Okay," she said. "I promised my new friend I'd make his uniform better than ever." She leaned forward and kissed Cat on the head. "Be a good cat, and I'll give you another treat when I get back."

Neither Neptune nor I said anything until the door swished shut behind her. "Did she just say she gave Cat treats?"

"She did."

We both looked back at Cat. Having built and rewired him, I knew how he was made. I knew how to access each panel, make repairs or upgrades, and switch him on and off. I also knew Cat wasn't a real cat. He didn't eat, and he didn't need a litter box. So what kind of treats had Pika been giving him?

I turned Cat around and tipped him so his face was looking up at me. The small panel under his chin that controlled his movement sensors wasn't secured properly. Using the end of my fingernail, I pried it loose. Whatever treats Pika had secretly been giving Cat were stuffed inside. I stuck my index finger and thumb into the narrow opening, and a stream of glitter poured out.

Neptune put his index finger in the powder and raised it to his nose. "She fed him one of Xina's powders," he said. "Will he still work?"

"I don't think that's all she fed him," I said. I jabbed my finger into the compartment and moved it around. Several glittery black rocks fell out. I picked one up and held it in my palm for Neptune to see. "Is that what I think it is?"

"It's a black diamond."

"It's not *a* black diamond. It's one of *the* black diamonds. That's why Xina was serving time. She was part of the team that stole these from the Intergalactic Supernova Museum."

"Her sentence doesn't fit that crime."

"She killed a security guard and was caught. The rest of her team got away. Either she's had these the whole time, or—"

"—or someone else involved in the crime is on Moon Unit 6."

And considering the value of the stolen collection of carbonado diamonds, it seemed like my question of motive had an answer.

37: STRANGE BEDFELLOWS

"Zeke said Xina fit a profile that matched your sister," I said. "He said she was released to engage you in a rescue mission."

"What does Zeke know about Xina?"

"He uploaded the junk DNA over her profile, remember? When he was in the computer, he saw the original files. I don't think he even knows he saw them, but I used a reliable method to retrieve the information from his temporary memory."

"What's this method?"

"I slapped him." Neptune wasn't fazed. "Twice."

"What else did he tell you?"

"She was in solitary for seven years and then moved to Colony 13 where she was serving out her sentence." Pieces of the puzzle clicked into place. "That's how you found her. You went to Cheung

Qidd for leads. That's how your name got into the transcripts with my dad. Qidd committed a lot of crimes against the galaxy before he was locked up. He knew about Vesta, didn't he? And the experiments on Venus?"

"There are entire parts of Venus that are under known pirate control. I used my resources to find out where Vesta might be, and those resources pointed me to Qidd."

One of those resources was my father. I knew it without asking. And I knew from how Neptune looked at me that he knew I knew. He'd been in touch with my dad and hadn't said a word. He reached for my wrist and I pulled my arm away.

"Don't waste time asking how I feel about you meeting with Jack Stryker," I said. "This is about your family. Not mine."

"Cheung Qidd provided the facilities on Venus where Federation Council conducted the experiments. The council knowingly entered into an agreement with a pirate. Qidd knew what was taking place and he profited. When I learned he could help me find Vesta, I agreed to his one request: to get Xina Astryd to Venus in exchange for his cooperation."

Something about Neptune's information didn't make sense. I ran the facts through my head over and over and considered the rest of the people we'd encountered on the ship since departing. "Xina was sick. She was going to die. It didn't matter if she had her chip removed or not."

Someone else on the ship knew about Xina. They either knew her real secret or her fake cover story. They either knew of her involvement in the diamond heist or thought she was related to Neptune. I still didn't know if her death was linked to him or not, and that made it difficult to determine our next move.

"What's Xina's relation to Qidd? Why would he care about getting her back to Venus?"

"Qidd doesn't care about Xina. He cares about the diamonds."

"You knew," I said slowly. "You said the doctor on Venus would remove her chip for a price. That's the price. You knew all along she had the diamonds, didn't you?"

He didn't speak. I felt my chest tighten at the thought that Neptune had been indirectly helping Cheung Qidd get stolen property. "Before he was arrested, Qidd was the most notorious pirate in the galaxy. How is it you can trust him? His band killed my mother. How can you ask *me* to trust him?"

"I don't. And I won't. But right now, Qidd's intel is all we have."

"Not exactly," I said. I shook the remaining glitter out of Cat's hollowed out opening and reattached the door panel. I spun him around and activated the data stream. His eyes glowed, projecting the images of two file folders onto Neptune's black uniform. I turned Cat to face the wall. The folders were labeled Neptune and Xina.

"Open Xina File," I said.

The folder icon opened, but the contents surprised me.

I'd never had reason to see files from Independent Border Patrol, but I would have expected them to contain background information, family and medical history, and arrest records. Pictures that illustrated the suspect. Possibly even a list of known aliases, open warrants, suspicious activities or identifying characteristics. But when I saw the contents of Xina's folder, I realized the IBP files meant nothing in context to what I knew about her, about the arrangement, and about her association with a notorious space pirate.

Because the contents of Xina's folder contained one line: *see Stryker*.

38: THE SPACE BAR

"Why does her file point to me?" I asked, more to myself than Neptune.

"Access your file," he said.

"I can't. I didn't copy it."

"But it exists?"

"Yes," I said. "When I got into Lumiere's computer, I first searched 'Stryker' to find out what his filing system was. Once I saw where he filed me, I knew how to access Xina's file."

"And mine. Open it."

"Forget I did that, okay?"

"Do it."

I opened Neptune's file and then stood directly in front of Cat so the information the robot projected distorted over my Stealthyester®. "You could have told me you went to Colony 13 to meet with my dad after Moon Unit 5. I assume you had good reason. You know stuff about him that I don't, and you never said a word. So yes, I accessed your file, because I want to know what you know. You could have told me, and you didn't."

All the anger that I hadn't admitted to myself, the anger over pretending I didn't care that Neptune had been in contact with my dad spilled out. Ever since the day he was arrested, I'd thought of my dad as a monster. I lost friends first. And then, I lost my family and planet. And Neptune knew the truth—a truth he wouldn't tell me. I'd been trying so hard to be the security team member I'd wanted to be, but I wasn't. I couldn't pretend none of this mattered. Not anymore. Whatever it was that was in Neptune's file, I didn't need to see.

I left. I didn't expect Neptune to charge after me. It's not like we were a couple in the middle of a fight. But just in case, I was going to make sure I couldn't be found. I took the HVPTS to Sector 3. Sector 3 to Sector 7. Sector 7 to Sector 9.

By the time I ended up at Sector 12, I was so jumbled I could barely see straight. It had taken less than a minute, and I doubted there was any way Neptune, or anybody, could have found me. I kept one hand on the wall for balance and stumbled forward. I was pretty sure the Space Bar was around here, and now that I'd recused myself from Neptune's mission, if nothing else, I deserved a drink.

On my way, I detected the sweet smell of sugar. As I rounded the corner, Synn and Shyrr strolled toward me. Synn had his arm around Shyrr, his fingertips resting on the small of her back. She stared straight ahead. Synn nodded at me, and I managed a feeble smile.

"Lieutenant Stryker, are you okay?" he asked.

"Yes, just a little wobbly. I'm sure some pure oxygen in the Space Bar will help."

"It's a small crowd tonight. Your friends will be happy to see you."

"I'm not meeting friends there," I said. "I just want to relax and enjoy some alone time before we reach Venus."

Shyrr flinched. Synn extended his arms so his hand curled around the side of her waist, and he pulled her closer to him. "Alone time is an unfamiliar concept," he said. "Venusians prefer the company of others."

My nerve endings tingled, and my temperature rose. This wasn't the first time Synn had hinted about the ways of Venus, and each time he said something like that I became uncomfortable. I tried to read Shyrr's expression, but she had turned slightly toward Synn, and her face was no longer visible. She clearly found comfort in closeness to her partner. Perhaps they were just being polite and wanted to leave.

"I should be moving on," I said. "Have a nice night."

Synn nodded once again, deliberately, and then the two of them continued down the hall. Faint sparkles trailed behind them. As I headed away, I heard a set of doors swoosh open and then shut.

I reached the Space Bar and took a seat inside the door. More than half of the tables were empty, and the lights were low. The dining and entertainment portion of the evening had passed, and restaurant crew had started clearing tables. I ordered a glass of Saturnian wine but let it go untouched when it arrived.

I wanted to shut off my brain, but I couldn't. Lumiere's files didn't make sense. I'd assumed he had files on everybody on the ship. But having Xina's file point to me presumed a connection between the two of us, which made zero sense. Before departure, I didn't know she existed.

I tried to remember that day. The day Xina's name had been announced as the winner of the Moon Unit Corporation publicity contest. I'd stood next to Neptune and watched from OB One while Xina accepted her passenger credentials right before an explosion of citron atoms and glitter had kicked off the festivities. Neptune had charged down to the platform to take control. But Lumiere had been there. He'd been guarding the exit and only left his post to hand me the transmitter that had fallen off my uniform. He'd also been the one to keep me from following Neptune. And he'd been the one to tell me the explosion was part of the celebration.

What else had I seen? Everyone planning to travel on the ship was on the platform: families, couples, and friends. I'd watched young Ellison chase Pika. Ellison, who'd thrown ice cream on my dress at First Dinner and on Ofra Starr's custom uniform. There shouldn't have been children on this trek because Venus was a couples' destination. It wasn't forbidden, but even Ofra had acknowledged it was an odd choice on the part of the parents.

What were his parents' names? Yesenia and George. They'd been at our table at First Dinner too. Captain Ryder, Officer Lumiere, Synn, Shyrr, and me. There had to be a reason the out-of-place family dressed in black instead of white had been seated with us. Either they'd paid for the privilege, or they were notable guests.

I waved Nyota over to my table. Despite the relaxed dress code at the Space Bar, the hostess was dressed formally. Tonight's dress was sleeveless teal jersey with an open back. Loose fabric swung around her legs when she walked.

"Hi, Nyota, I'm Lieutenant Stryker from the uniform ward."

"I remember you. That kid threw ice cream on

your dress at First Dinner." She pointed over her shoulder. "I got it out with some good old club soda. It's in the kitchen. Do you want me to get it for you?"

I shook my head. "Not right now. You remember that night—do you remember my table?"

"Sure. You were with the captain."

"Yes. You know the family that was seated with us? The parents and the little boy—Ellison—who threw the colored ice at me?"

"That kid's a real troublemaker. He turned the valve on the nitrous oxide after you left, and I had to send half my staff to their quarters to sleep off the laughing gas."

"Who is he?"

"That was Ambassador Yesenia Reeves and her attaché, George. Ellison is George's son. Last minute thing from what I heard. His mother wasn't available to make the trip and George didn't have any choice but to bring his kid."

I was more interested in Yesenia's role. "Ambassador to what?"

"Federation Council Ambassador to Venus."

"A representative from FC has been on the ship this whole time?"

"Yes. Why? You look scared. You didn't do something illegal, did you?" She laughed. "That's why she asked Captain Ryder to keep her identity quiet. George and Ellison help make them look like a family."

Nyota got called to another table. I sipped my wine and thought about what that might mean. If it were Ambassador Reeves's vacation, she would not have brought along her attaché and his son. This was a job. She was going to Venus for a reason.

That's why Lumiere was on the ship too. He was overseeing the transport of precious cargo. That precious cargo was a person. A person who would not be allowed on a Moon Unit cruise ship because she was a prisoner. A prisoner like Xina Astryd, who Neptune had agreed to help in exchange for finding his sister.

They all knew about Xina's true identity. Any one of them could have gotten to her whenever they wanted. And maybe it was in Federation Council's best interests to terminate Xina before reaching Venus to keep relations between planets as they were or to keep her evidence of their cross-breeding experiment secret. Maybe they knew she'd been traveling with the stolen diamonds and wanted to make sure the booty didn't end up in the hands of the pirates. This wasn't a private Neptune mission; it was a Federation Council mission. And the only person who didn't know the truth was Neptune.

I left the Space Bar. Between the alcohol in the wine and the after-effects of taking five rapid trips on the HVPTS, I was not fully operational. I didn't have to get far. One last trip on the HVPTS to get to security section and tell Neptune what I knew, and I could crash in my room.

I rounded the corner and saw Ellison sitting in the middle of the hallway. He wore a hooded shearling robe with a blanket bunched up around him and sat on the orange carpet with his back to me, his legs in a V in front of him. I kept my hand on the wall for stabilization and cleared my throat to announce my presence.

As I got closer, I saw he was playing with a robotic pet, not unlike the toy Cat was. I slowed and squatted behind him. "Hi, Ellison. Does your dad know you're out here?" I asked.

The boy turned to face me, and a hint of green skin peeked from under his shearling hood. He wasn't Ellison after all. He was a Martian in sheep's clothing.

39: GREEN WITH ENVY

I stood up too fast, and the hallway spun. The hood fell back on the robe and Bottol, the meanest of the Martians, stared out. His pupils were dilated to a disturbing size, appearing as large, unfocused, vacant orbs. "You have the rest of them," he said. "Where are they?"

"What?"

"The diamonds," he said. He opened his palm, and several rough black stones glistened in his glove. "We stole hundreds. Where are the rest of them?"

"*You* stole hundreds?" I stepped away from him. "You—you killed Xina?"

"Xina died the day she was arrested for killing a guard. Her life was over. She should have told me where she put the diamonds when I attacked her in the hallway in front of your ward. If she had given them to me, I would have let her live out the rest of her short life." He laughed.

"But Xina died from a head wound," I said. "She was twice your size. How—"

"Stop it!" Bottol cried out. "You all underestimate me. I could have killed you when you were face down on the carpet."

"You knocked her down and struck her head," I said slowly. Nobody would have suspected a Martian of inflicting a head wound on a seven-foot-tall Venusian. Even I'd only viewed the Martians as a nuisance, not a threat. If I'd made my report like I should have, Bottol would be locked up and not blocking my exit from Sector 12.

"You've been snooping around Xina enough to know where the rest of the diamonds are. You and that pink pet of yours. Give them to me," he demanded.

The facts snapped into place. Bottol was part of the team that had robbed Federation Council of the priceless black diamonds, but because Xina killed a security guard, the heat had crashed down on them all and he'd never seen a penny from the heist. She'd been arrested but had kept the diamonds hidden. Neptune was getting her to Venus in exchange for her help freeing his real sister. And even though Xina was dying from the malfunctioning chip in her head, Bottol had been mad enough to kill her when he had the chance.

I took two additional steps backward. Bottol stood and charged me unexpectedly. He was small but compact, and the impact made me stumble back several steps until I reached the wall. "Don't make me fight you, Bottol. You know I'll win."

"I wouldn't get too confident." He removed a small canister from under his robe and pulled the pin. He slipped a round metal ring onto the top of the canister and pushed it down, pressing the trigger and holding it in the spray position. A thin mist of gas spread in the hallway, expanding like a nebula throughout space.

I reached into the neck of my Stealthyester® turtleneck and pulled out the thin tube that connected to the oxygen canister strapped to my thigh. I fed the tube into my mouth and inhaled deeply and then lowered my center of gravity for better balance. Bottol was surprised but not scared. He grabbed my ankles and yanked. Through determination or strength he'd held in reserve, he pulled my feet out from under me and I slammed down onto the floor.

He was a little green alien man. I was a big purple half alien woman. Bets on the outcome of our fight would have been split.

Bottol scrambled onto me and sliced through the cord attached to my oxygen tube with a small knife blade. I pushed him away, sending him across the hall. He fell into a door and grunted. I tried to stand but was too dizzy and only made it halfway. Bottol grabbed his canister and aimed it at my head. I held my breath. The gas spread through the hallway. It was less potent than before but more infernal. My lungs convulsed. I dropped back down to my hands and knees and crawled to the closest door. I was too low to the ground to activate the door open sensors. I slapped my hand on the exterior surface and choked out a cry for help. There was no answer.

My brain was cloudy and my muscles sluggish, but I focused on the principles of self-defense Mattix Dusk had taught me. It was never about strike and be struck. It was about the movement of energy. Circles. Flow. Water. Balance. I closed my eyes and inhaled. Exhaled. Opened my eyes and moved to the center of the hallway. I squatted, centering my core over my feet, and stared at Bottol.

He laughed. "Don't be pathetic, Plunian," he said. "I can beat you when you're standing at full height. You don't need to sink to my level."

"I'd never sink to your level," I said. "You stole from people who dedicated their lives to protecting the galaxy. You bullied a Gremlon who never learned how to defend herself. You killed the one person who could help reunite a family."

"What you know about family could fit on a microorganism," he said.

As the gas filled the hallway, my brain grew cloudier. I couldn't let Bottol know. I had to hold my position and conserve my energy. Wait until he struck and use his strength against him. I couldn't let him bait me with insults and trash talk about my dad.

"You'll never get the diamonds," I said. "All this time they were right under your nose. Or should I say over your nose? What's it like going through life knowing everything is over your head?"

It was the right gamble. Martians were sensitive about their height and were known to be dirty fighters, and Bottol was no different. If he had reinforcements coming, they were going to miss the main event.

He charged toward me. I braced myself for impact. He struck. I curled into a ball and rolled in a backward somersault. The force, plus my low resistance, kept him moving at a speed he couldn't control. He hit the wall at the end of the hallway, his small green hands splayed out on either side of his face. He turned and bared his teeth. A bruise formed on the upper left of his sizeable green forehead. He balled his hands into fists and charged me again. This time I rolled to the side of the hallway at the last minute and Bottol flew past me.

I was aware that I couldn't do this forever. Bottol was unaffected by the gas that was slowly draining me. I needed help. There was none. No one knew where I was. If anyone went looking for me, the dead-end hallway on the outside of the HVPTS Sector 12 landing pad was the last place they'd think to check. And after all my complaining about the comm device, I recognized the value of having someone listening to my every move.

That's when I spotted the toy Bottol had been playing with in the hallway. It wasn't like Cat; it *was* Cat. Bottol had taken the small robotic feline apart in search of the diamonds. Only I knew how Cat worked, but Pika had treated him like a real cat and fed him treats on top of his vocal chip. We'd found some of the diamonds inside him. He may not meow like he used to, but that might be okay. If Neptune found Cat in the HVPTS he'd know something was wrong.

I tucked Cat between my chin and chest and crawled toward the transport tube.

"Forget it, Plunian!"

I dropped Cat and head-butted him into the chamber. Bottol grabbed my ankles and dragged me backward away from the HPVTS. The door sealed, and Cat launched to another part of the ship. Which one, I had no idea.

The principles of harmony and energy left my brain, and I clawed at Bottol, trying to get him off of me. He jabbed his knife at my Stealthyester® leggings, like tiny stings over my calves. I was fading. I closed my eyes for a moment to regroup.

The rush of the HVPTS sounded. I opened my eyes and looked up. Had Cat been too light to trigger the door release? Had the unit returned him to me?

A man in an unfamiliar baggy black uniform stepped out. He aimed his space gun at Bottol and fired. Bottol's entire body flinched with the impact and then went limp.

I kicked my legs until they were out from under the Martian's body and then used my soles to push away from him. When my back was against the wall, I stood. I slowly looked up from Bottol's body to see the face of the man who'd saved me. He had purple skin, wise eyes, and enough lines in his face to put him thirty-some years older than me. Recognition hit like an asteroid crashing into Earth, and I put both hands out on the wall for support.

"Dad?"

40: FATHER FIGURE

"THERE'S NO TIME TO EXPLAIN," THE MAN SAID. He lifted Bottol from the carpet and headed back to the HVPTS. Halfway in, he turned around and said, "I'm proud of you, Sylvia." And then, in the next moment, he was gone.

"No!" I yelled. I ran to the transport tube and slapped my hand against the exterior. The pressure reset, and the door opened. Empty. In seconds, my dad had been back in my life and then gone. I climbed on and closed my eyes, trying to feel the comfort of family, but all I felt was alone in a plastic tube.

"He is not gone forever."

Shyrr stood outside the tube. She extended her hand toward me. I took it and stepped out. "Come with me," she said. "I have oxygen."

We walked to the door that I'd pounded on

while fighting with Bottol. The doors opened. Cool, crisp air filled the room. I gulped in breaths until my faculties returned.

"Thank you," I said.

"I have done nothing but stand by and watch. I have not helped. I was too afraid. You fought well. You are lucky to have one who trains and protects you."

"My father didn't protect me. My life is what it is because he lied about everything."

"Your father is like my brother," she said. "He has made decisions to protect others instead of himself."

"Synn is your brother? He's been protecting you this whole time?"

"Synn is my guard. He was employed on this trip to ensure my safe travel to Venus."

"But you said your brother—" I studied Shyrr's face, her iridescent skin and wideset eyes. All this time she'd been on the ship right in front of us. I'd mocked Bottol for things being over his head, and here was the most obvious answer that I'd failed to see all along. "You are Neptune's sister," I said. "Your real name is Vesta."

"Yes."

"He said he wanted to rescue you."

"Yes. He found me on Colony 7. I told him of the others. Those who did not escape Venus. I have enjoyed a life the others never knew. Neptune agreed to help me seek their release by trading for their lives."

I didn't ask what Neptune was going to trade. I didn't have to. There were two things of value on Moon Unit 6: the diamonds stolen from Federation Council and Xina Astryd. I now understood why Neptune had sought an audience with Cheung Qidd in prison. Neptune would have wanted to know what was worth the price of the lives of the Venusian slaves. Qidd may have been incarcerated for life, but that didn't mean he was without power or greed. Pirates valued property and revenge. And Neptune could deliver both.

The door to Shyrr's room swished open, and Neptune's large frame filled the opening. The light in the hallway backlit him and kept him in silhouette.

"Neptune, Shyrr, you two have a lot to talk about." I walked toward the door, expecting Neptune to move out of the way. The closer I got, the brighter the glow coming off my body.

"Stryker," Neptune said.

"Save your words for your sister." I turned and looked back at Shyrr, who smiled at us both. "You two have to work out what happens when you reach Venus."

I left them, climbed into the HVPTS, and headed to Medi-Bay where Doc admitted me immediately.

I survived. Bottol did not. The ray fired from the space gun shouldn't have been strong enough to kill, but Bottol had taken an almost lethal amount of prescription medication stolen from Medi-Bay while being treated for the contaminated protein pack thing. All along I'd suspected that Neptune or Zeke had something to do with the tainted protein packs, but that turned out to be the Martians too. It was Bottol's way of creating an alibi for Xina's murder and the others had fallen in line when he promised them the chance to raid Doc's cabinet of medications.

Doc was not amused.

I'd been right about so many little things but wrong about one major one. Yes, the captain, Lumiere, and Federation Council all knew about Neptune's mission, but their presence wasn't because of Xina Astryd. It was because of Jack Stryker. It was his file I'd accessed in Officer Lumiere's database when learning his file naming conventions. "See Stryker" meant him, not me. Nobody would tell me details. But the sentence I heard, over and over, was this: "It's not what you think."

They didn't know what I thought, so how could they say that?

I could have saved a lot of stress on this trip if I'd known Anatol wouldn't make a report on Xina's murder. As second in command, he was aware that Moon Unit 6 was cooperating with Federation Council in the transport of a prisoner to Venus. He, like me, just didn't know which one.

It was Border Patrol who took possession of Xina's body. When Lumiere woke from his Mickey, he suspected he'd been played. He just didn't know why. He instructed a member of the body disposal team to move Xina's body to his quarters where he could guarantee it wouldn't be tampered with. Sadly for him, the smell guaranteed he'd spend the rest of the trip alone.

Lucky for me, the medic transferred Ofra's uniform from Xina's body to the medical dummy and left the dummy on the cart where Zeke had found it.

No one had been interested in the murder of a prisoner but me. Involving Zeke, though a good idea at the time, had created complications Neptune hadn't foreseen. But having Zeke's repair pod available in case of emergency had been worth it. When Moon Unit 6 arrived at Venus, both Bottol and Xina's bodies were removed from the ship in secret while the rest of the passengers disembarked for their two days of fun. Moon Unit Corporation promised Zeke a substantial reward for his help in protecting their image. I knew Zeke would take the money, but I wasn't sure how he'd handle the return trip with Neptune in his repair pod. Or how he'd explain the whole thing to his dad when they landed.

Not my problem.

While the rest of the crew took two days leave in Venus, I stayed behind. Mostly for my twice daily check-ins with Doc, but also to get the uniform ward back up to standard. And keep Pika company.

And try to figure out what she had done with the diamonds.

Neptune had turned over the small quantity of the valuable black gems that Pika had hidden in Cat, and while we knew that was only a portion of what had been boosted during the original crime, Federation Council accepted that they might never recover the rest. Once on the black market, the stones would be impossible to track. When I was finally granted private council with Ambassador Reeves, I learned that recovery of the gemstones was not the council's top priority.

"Our mission is peace," she said. "We mistakenly believed the gems were a symbol of that rarest of commodities. We now know they were merely a source of corruption. To focus on corruption is to sacrifice our intended goals."

I didn't know how their goals involved my dad, but I would find out. And if I had the diamonds as leverage, all the better. I combed through Xina's quarters four times and ran program after program to see if Cat had picked up any data. I badgered Pika who, in classic Gremlon fashion, didn't remember what she'd done with them. "I don't have anything that doesn't belong to me," she said over and over again.

And you know what? I believed her.

EPILOGUE: BRIGHT FUTURE

I stood on Observation Deck One, watching the passengers of Moon Unit 6 leave the ship. There were no canisters of citron cartridges ready to explode and send us off in a burst of energy. In place of the manufactured fanfare, a genuine camaraderie had developed. I was unaccustomed to the attention from colleagues congratulating me on the return flight or consoling me over the encounter with Bottol. The other Martians, the ones not part of his mean green team, looked the other way when they passed me, no doubt embarrassed at how a few bad apples could spoil the whole bunch. Lumiere avoided eye contact too, for entirely different reasons. Daila congratulated me on a job well done. Doc slipped me a salesman's sample of Anti-Vert pills. And Ellison chased Pika around the docking pad.

As I watched, I tried to get a handle on how I felt. I didn't know. I was scared and angry and surprised and shocked.

Mostly shocked. Doc told me to call him anytime, and I was pretty sure he meant it as an order, not a nicety. Maybe I would; maybe I wouldn't. I wasn't sure what I was going to do next.

"Stryker."

I'd expected that voice. I turned around and faced Neptune. "How'd everything go on Venus?" I asked.

"That's classified."

I rolled my eyes. "Is there such a thing as being a part of a mission and actually finding out whether it was successful? Or does that not happen? Because I think that should happen. I bet morale in security section would rise *exponentially* if that happened."

"I read your report." He pursed his lips. "We're going to have to work on your communication skills before the next trip."

"At least I say more than 'Go' when I want to engage in conversation."

I stared at him, and he stared back. In terms of ally or enemy, I'd rather have him on my team than working against me, but I still didn't know how to categorize him. Could I trust him? He'd trusted me and look how that had turned out.

I leaned on the rail and stared at the departing

crew. A few smiled at me. Ofra Starr, dressed in a newly cleaned uniform exited the ship. He looked up and waved. I waved back. He pointed at his shirt and then gave me a thumbs up. I had to admit, his uniform looked good. Radiant. Under the bright rays of the full sun, he glowed.

I leaned closer to the glass, practically pressing my nose against the window. Ofra's uniform was trimmed in small black stones by the cuffs and hem. Pika had promised to make his uniform better than ever, and with the secret stash of stolen Federation Council diamonds, she certainly delivered on that promise.

"Is Ofra glowing?" Neptune asked.

"He's just naturally radiant," I said. I turned my back on the window and leaned against the rail.

"Pika," he said. And then he smiled a full smile. It was an expression I'd only seen hints of during previous moon treks, and I wasn't prepared for how it changed his face. His teeth were white against his skin, and an unexpected gleam sparkled in his eyes. "Stryker, keep a tail on Ofra Starr during the break between Moon Unit trips."

"Who says I'm staying with Moon Unit Corporation?"

"You can't quit. You know too much."

"What if I don't want this life? What if I want to walk away?"

Neptune grabbed my wrist, and my skin

glowed almost immediately. We were nowhere near Venus. He made a point of looking at my arm and then at my face. "I think we both know you're not walking away."

"What about you?" I said. "You lost everything the last time you got involved with a subordinate."

"You're not a subordinate, Stryker. You're an equal. You just need to finish your training."

I felt a rush of heat through me. "This training. Where exactly is it going to take place? I don't know where I'll be two days from now."

Neptune tapped his ear.

"You can't contact me via the comm device. Doc took it out, remember?"

A burst of static sounded in my ear, followed by Zeke Champion's voice. "Um, Sylvia? I'm pretty sure Neptune convinced Doc to put it back in while you were recovering."

"Neptune did what?" I looked up at Neptune.

He raised an eyebrow. "I'll be in touch," he said.

SATURN NIGHT FEVER

Keep reading for an excerpt from *Saturn Night Fever*, Sylvia Stryker's next novel adventure!

IMPACT

When Neptune said I fought like a girl, I did the only respectable thing. I hit him. That's not to say it's a good idea for dropouts from the space academy to strike their newly-appointed superiors, but in this case, he deserved it.

In the two versions of the story that will be told of the incident, at least one will contain the fact that technically, I was in training. Technically, the only reason we were on the helipad on the corner of Neptune's property was because the helipad was a convenient place to practice. Technically, I was being paid a small sponsorship fee to test the durability of new uniforms designed for Moon Unit Corporation, and technically, the only way I could fully know if the uniforms were durable were to see how they held up when I threw a punch.

Neptune's version might include slight variations.

"In case you haven't noticed, I *am* a girl," I said.

Neptune was bigger, older, and more experienced than I was, and he probably had more important things to do than spend the day teaching me defensive maneuvers. But never graduating had left me with relatively few channels to advance my learning.

After Moon Unit 6 returned from Venus, Neptune contacted me via the comm device implanted in my ear and offered me free room and board in exchange for lessons to pick up where my interrupted education had left off. I'd dropped out when my dad was arrested so I could help my mom with the family dry ice mines. Neptune's offer to teach me gave us both something of value. I'd accepted, more for me than for him. I'm selfish that way.

"You know why you were almost incapacitated on our last moon trek?" he asked. "Because you dropped your guard. You thought size and skill were enough to beat your enemy. You fought fair. You fought like a woman."

"Oh, so now I'm a woman?" I countered. "I grew up fast."

It wasn't that Neptune treated me like a girl or a woman. He treated me like a student. And most of the time I was okay with that. But the voice in my head that I didn't want to listen to wondered why someone like Neptune spent time training someone like me. It was a voice that hadn't had much to question since my dad was arrested.

Any attention paid to me usually had strings attached. Retribution for my dad's crimes, or the novelty of my half Plunian background in a world where lavender women were now rare. More than once I'd fended off advances when I saw where they were headed. I developed a thick skin and narrowed my social circle to a very tight group.

But despite the fact that Neptune was a muscular wall of taciturn authority, or maybe because of it, I was attracted to him. I doubted it was the black military-issue cargo gear he wore (did he buy his clothes in bulk?) or the intimidating stance he'd perfected long before I met him (arms crossed, feet shoulder-width apart). I'd never been attracted to men in power—in fact, power was a pretty tried-and-true turn-*off*. I didn't know what it was about Neptune that made my lavender skin glow at the least opportune times. I only knew it was important to me to prove to him that I was different. Today, different meant throwing a non-girly punch.

He grabbed my wrist and closed my fingers into a fist. His hand was twice the size of mine—tawny against my lavender coloring. "You have to toughen up, Stryker. You're smart, and you learn information fast, but instincts don't come from a book."

"I learned how to fight by an accredited Hapkido master. Or have you already forgotten that I dropped you with a sweeping kick because you underestimated me?"

He let go of my fist and pointed at me. "Don't let that go to your head. Success is built on failure. If you learn anything from these lessons, learn that. Failure is your friend."

"I thought failure wasn't an option? The flight director of Earth's space shuttle program said it, right? His biography was required reading."

"You didn't read the book. That's a made-up quote from a movie script. The flight director liked the line so much he used it for the title of his biography. Lesson number two: check your source. I thought you knew that by now."

I didn't tell Neptune that I hadn't read the book because the course took place after I dropped out. I'm pretty sure lesson number three was to keep your weaknesses to yourself.

"Repeat it back to me."

"Blah, blah, check your source."

"Repeat what I told you about failure."

"'Failure is my friend.'"

"Remember that." He turned around and walked a few feet away from me and then turned back. "If you think you can fight because you dropped me—once—then you'll get complacent. Don't forget what happened the last time you got complacent."

How could I forget? I almost died. It didn't help that the fight had been four against one or that my oxygen supply had been cut off, rendering me helpless. My opponents knew my weakness and used it against me. Nothing fair about it. I didn't want to admit it, but Neptune was right. I'd falsely assumed I could defend myself without too much effort, and my false sense of confidence had worked against me.

"Go again," he said. He bent his knees slightly and prepared for my attack. I swung my arms forward and backward, giant half circles to limber up my shoulders, and felt a seam tear. "Hold on. Uniform malfunction. Moon Unit Corporation thinks they can cut corners by using a different supplier, but the last six uniforms I tested fell apart."

"Where?"

"Shoulder." I turned and pointed to where I'd felt the split. "What am I supposed to tell them this time? 'Looks good but you can't throw a girly punch'?"

I felt Neptune tug the split fabric together. Even though I wasn't looking at him, just the graze of his fingertips against my shoulder blade made me flush.

"Why are you wasting your time with uniforms?"

"Someday the name 'Sylvia Stryker' will be synonymous with space uniforms. After our trip to Venus, the publicity company who planned the hype around the Moon Units contacted me to wear test their prototypes. It's a little cash on the side between treks and all things considered, I can use the money. I can't crash here forever."

I knew Neptune wouldn't pursue the conversation. He understood my predicament: no planet, no family, no home. He was with me the night space pirates destroyed everything I'd ever known. The only reason I agreed to train with him was because there's a certain security in spending time with someone who prioritized silence over small talk. I could learn a lot from Neptune and I knew it.

He could learn from me too. I wasn't sure he knew that. Yet.

Neptune's loner lifestyle suited him, but I was glad that he begrudgingly allowed me to coexist on his property. Not one to mooch, I made sure to bring what I could to the table. Enter Mattix Dusk, space courier (and my Hapkido instructor) who traveled between the thirteen colonies under Federation Control, to pick up and deliver anything that needed to be picked up or delivered. I introduced the two men and they worked out a mutually acceptable deal. Mattix had use of the helipad and a place to crash while on the Kuiper Belt. Neptune had access to Mattix's courier contacts and suppliers. And for the foreseeable future, I had not one but two mentors who could further my education.

Where Neptune was tall, tawny, and solid muscle, Mattix looked like a piece of worn leather in loose-fitting castoff clothes. Tanned skin, bleached hair worn in a ponytail, and ragamuffin clothes suited him. His job as courier put him in front of shady characters, and he passed along his two most important pieces of advice: look like you have less than the other guy and learn to take care of yourself.

Whatever direction my lesson was supposed to go was interrupted by a swiftly approaching space pod. I looked at the sky and watched it glide toward us. It was the Dusk Driver, the space pod that belonged to Mattix.

I smiled and waved while backing up so he could land. As his space pod drew closer, alarm bells rang out from the nearby towers. His speed was too fast. He was going to crash. And if I didn't get out of the way, I'd burn up in the wreckage.

Neptune reached the same conclusion before I did. How do I know? When I tore my attention from the incoming space pod to tell Neptune something was wrong, I saw him charge toward me. The impact knocked me to the ground.

Either Neptune knew what was happening and wanted to save me, or he was trying to make a point.

From the bank of dirt alongside the helipad, the space pod jerked to a halt and then hovered two feet above the ground. Mattix knew better than to approach at the speed he had, but he'd compensated for the potential accident by activating the ship's invisible buffer: a two foot "bumper" of static electricity that kept the exterior from contacting another surface. It operated much the same way as two magnets held in close proximity. The dueling forcefields pushed away from each other, making it impossible to touch. Mattix wouldn't have activated the buffer shield unless something was wrong.

I scrambled to my feet and, keeping my center of gravity low, approached the space pod. Mattix wouldn't allow anyone else to navigate the ship without reason, which made what I saw even scarier.

The ship was being flown on autopilot.

ACKNOWLEDGMENTS

Thank you to:

The readers who embraced my idea to set a mystery series in outer space! Your acceptance of Sylvia and her world have given me an entirely new playground.

The members of Shoptalk, my Facebook group, for answering my last-minute call for help when I discovered I named two characters the same thing. You outdid yourselves in a very short amount of time!

Eva Hartmann of Your Fiction Editor for seeing what it was I wanted to do and helping me get there. "Muscular wall of taciturn authority" is all you.

Bananarama and Tom Jones: for putting a song in my head that I liked well enough to use as a title.

The following for contributions to the general

catalog of space-themed pop-culture that continues to inspire me every day: Gene Roddenberry, *Star Trek*, Gerry and Sylvia Anderson, J. J. Abrams, George Lucas, and the team that brought us *Galaxy Quest*.

...and a recent binge of Billy Jack movies, which led directly to Sylvia being trained in Hapkido.

ABOUT THE AUTHOR

National bestselling author Diane Vallere writes funny and fashionable character-based novels. After two decades working for a top luxury retailer, she traded fashion accessories for accessories to murder in her first book, *Designer Dirty Laundry*. A past president of Sisters in Crime, Diane started her own detective agency at age ten and has maintained a passion for shoes, clues, and clothes ever since.

(The outer space angle came when she was eleven.)

ALSO BY

Samantha Kidd Mysteries

Designer Dirty Laundry

Buyer, Beware

The Brim Reaper

Some Like It Haute

Grand Theft Retro

Pearls Gone Wild

Cement Stilettos

Panty Raid

Union Jacked

Slay Ride

Tough Luxe

Fahrenheit 501

Madison Night Mad for Mod Mysteries

"Midnight Ice" Novella

Pillow Stalk

That Touch of Ink

With Vics You Get Eggroll

The Decorator Who Knew Too Much

The Pajama Frame

Lover Come Hack

Apprehend Me No Flowers

Teacher's Threat

The Kill of it All

Sylvia Stryker Outer Space Mysteries

Fly Me To The Moon

I'm Your Venus

Saturn Night Fever

Spiders from Mars

Material Witness Mysteries

Suede to Rest

Crushed Velvet

Silk Stalkings

Costume Shop Mystery Series

A Disguise to Die For

Masking for Trouble

Dressed to Confess

Mermaid Mysteries

Tails from the Deep

Murky Waters

Sleeping with the Fishes

Non-Fiction

Bonbons For Your Brain

Made in the USA
Las Vegas, NV
23 July 2021